Mythil's Secret

Mythil's Secret

Prashani Rambukwella

Popsicle Books

COLOMBO

Published by Popsicle Books, 2009
an imprint of the Perera Hussein Publishing House
www.ph-books.com

ISBN: 978-955-0041-00-8

First edition

To offset the environmental pollution caused by printing books,
the Perera Hussein Publishing House grows trees in Puttalam –
Sri Lanka's semi-arid zone

Layout by Hanim AbdulCader
Printed and bound in Sri Lanka by Samayawardhana

Contents

Recipe for trouble

'Go outside and play Mythil.'

Who am I supposed to play with anyway, Mythil thought to himself as he stalked angrily out of his parents' room. It was always the same. Every time his parents were about to fight they would send Mythil outside. And they seemed to be fighting all the time now. They argued about the shopping. They quibbled about who had used the phone most and run up the phone bill. They even yelled at Mythil if he forgot to switch off a light when he left a room.

He stood for a minute in the corridor that connected all the bedrooms of Archchi's old house. The ornate yaka masks that hung on the wall looked back at him impassively. Then as his parents voices grew louder he stamped his foot, pulled a face at the masks and walked away.

They were visiting his grandmother for the school holidays. Like most grandmothers Archchi was a favourite among her grandchildren and Mythil loved her more than anyone else in the world.

But Archchi's house stood deep down a leafy lane away from the village at the end of the vast stretch of communal paddy fields. There were no other children he could play with there. And there was no computer or television either. His cousins usually visited during the holidays but this time their parents couldn't take leave so he was all alone.

Mythil peeped in at his grandmother's room at the front of the house. Archchi was still having her afternoon nap. Otherwise he could have asked her to tell him a story or play a game of cards with him. He turned back along the corridor and paused outside his parents' room. He could hear his mother's angry voice.

'All I am saying is that we could have bought apple juice for her,' Ammi said. 'You know how much my mother likes it. And we're staying here for another week – living off her food . . .'

'When was the last time we bought apple juice for ourselves? Or for Mythil? It's expensive! We can't afford it!' That was his father's voice. 'If you think we're living off your mother's food I'll go out and buy five kilos of rice. That's a much better thing to spend money on than apple juice!' Thaththi sounded furious too.

Ammi laughed scornfully. 'She doesn't *need* rice! She gets it from her fields. That's why I said that instead of spending money on something like rice we should get her something she likes ...'

Mythil walked away shaking his head. Why did they have to fight about something trivial like apple juice? What was wrong with them? Did they hate each other so much that they had to fight about everything?

He headed for the pantry looking for something to eat. Archchi's house was a sprawling H-shaped bungalow surrounded by garden. The dining room and pantry, flanked by verandas, stood in the middle. The bedrooms formed one of the long lines of the H, while the hall, his grandfather's study and the kitchen formed the other. A little apart from the kitchen but in line with the H shape stood the shed.

Opening two of the many kevili-filled tins and containers on the dresser Mythil picked out one sweet kevili – an aluwa, and one savoury kevili – a crunchy kokis. He could see two of Archchi's cats sunning themselves in the kitchen yard outside. They were scaredy-cats that ran away if anyone other than Archchi or Seeli the cook approached. Mythil had a feeling that the cats only made friends with Seeli because she threw them scraps while she was cooking. They didn't jump on Seeli's lap purring the way they did with Archchi.

Breaking off a few crispy pieces of kokis he held them out in one hand and walked towards the cats going 'Puss, puss, puss,' like Seeli did. But the cats shot away from him. Mythil sighed. He popped the kokis pieces into his mouth and wondered what to do.

Seeli appeared from the kitchen with a large cane laundry basket under her arm. 'Where are you going at this time, Podi Baby?' she called out. He stuck his tongue out at her as she disappeared around the side of the house. Mythil hated when she called him 'Podi Baby' – little master. It wasn't his fault he was the youngest of the cousins. Perhaps he could pretend to be a bandit and follow her. He knew she was going towards the clothes lines strung out in a grove of fruit trees at the side of the house.

Carefully slipping the kevili into the pocket of his green army shorts he sidled along the shed wall until he was looking out at the side garden. Seeli was taking down the washed clothes and dumping them, loosely folded, into the cane basket. She had her back to Mythil so, crouching low over the grass, he ran and hid behind a large delum bush that grew beside one of the guava trees. Seeli didn't notice. She was humming along to a pop-song that could be heard playing from the tinny little battery operated radio she kept in her kitchen.

Mythil smothered a giggle as Seeli, who was rather plump, swayed to the music and threw a bed-sheet into the basket with a flourish. A mischievous thought entered his head. While Seeli was wrestling with a curtain Mythil scampered towards the laundry basket and threw the sheet over his head. Through the thin cotton material he could easily see Seeli unpegging the stubborn curtain in the bright afternoon sunlight. As soon as she turned towards the basket with the curtain in her arms Mythil leaped up with a menacing roar. Seeli gave a small scream and threw the curtain at him. It landed on the grass next to the basket. With a yelp of laughter Mythil shot out from under the sheet and ran away to the other side of the garden, towards the stream.

'Podi Baby!' Seeli yelled after him clutching her chest. 'What a fright you gave me! You wait! I'll tell your mother!'

Mythil hid behind a big kottamba tree near the stream and peeped out to see whether Seeli was chasing him. Satisfied that she wasn't, he sat on a rock that jutted out over the swift running water. He wasn't worried that Seeli would tell his mother about how he had scared her. Seeli wasn't a tattle-tale. And that was a good thing. The last thing he wanted was to have his parents angry at him as well as each other.

Pulling the kevili out of his pocket he crunched on the rest of the kokis. A branch overhead shaded him from the shimmering heat. He looked across the stream at the jungle – the jungle that teamed with pythons, poachers and yaka spirits, he thought dreamily.

Seeli called this the 'yakku gas nagina velawa,' which meant the time when even the yakas or nature spirits of the jungle climbed into the cool leafy branches of the trees to rest from the afternoon heat. It was the time when snakes came out of their holes to hunt and the jungle trembled in silent anticipation.

Mythil finished his kokis and brooded over his parents. Why did they have to keep fighting all the time? Why had they got married if they didn't love each other? He popped the aluwa into his mouth and let its sweetness melt over his tongue. Looking out across the stream Mythil half hoped he'd see a poacher or perhaps a yaka. That would be something exciting to distract him from worrying about his parents.

He was rinsing his fingers in the water when a movement in the jungle caught his eye. A figure was picking its way among the trees. Mythil felt his heart beat rapidly. Was it a poacher? He strained his eyes trying to make out the shadowy form. Then he sighed in relief as the person walked clear of the trees and waded across the stream. It was just Jamis the old gardener with an armload of firewood. The sullen old man ignored the boy and disappeared around the side of the house. Soon Mythil heard Jamis cutting the dry branches into smaller bits for the kitchen fire.

He watched a yellow jak leaf float down the stream and threw a stone at it. He missed hitting it by about a foot. On the other bank a pond heron took off in alarm, the white under its wings showing as it flew. Mythil watched it glide over the house. How different Hewagolla was from Colombo. When they were at home in Colombo he didn't have a big garden to play in. Or a stream to throw stones at. Or a brooding jungle just bristling with adventure.

And yet in other ways it was just like home. He had no one to play with here either. At home Thaththi was always working on the computer and Ammi was always teaching large groups of children. Ammi and Thaththi didn't seem to have time for him. And when they did get together at meal times his parents almost always argued. They were usually a little better when they were out on holiday at Archchi's but this time not even that seemed to be working. Mythil wished his cousins and uncles and aunts were here too.

I should run away and get kidnapped by poachers, Mythil thought to himself as he threw another stone at the stream. Maybe that would give them something else to think of rather than what they could argue about next.

The more he thought about it the better the idea seemed. Wasn't that what kids in movies did? They ran away from home or got kidnapped and then their parents were forced to work together to get them back and eventually fell in love again. Then he thought of Archchi and felt sorry. She would worry if he disappeared. She was the only person in the world who loved him. If only she didn't have to sleep in the afternoons.

He got up and ran back towards the house to check on her. Perhaps she was up now. Perhaps he could include her in the plan so that he could sneak back to the house for food if he got very hungry. Mythil imagined himself spending months in the jungle dressed in animal skins and carrying a bow and arrow like Sura Saradiyel or Robin Hood. He smiled to himself. Now that would be an adventure.

He took a roundabout route to Archchi's window, jumping carefully over her beloved clumps of anthuriums and looking back to make sure they were all right. He wanted to avoid coming within hearing distance of his parents' room.

He pulled himself up on to the ledge beneath Archchi's window and peered through the iron bars. Archchi still lay fast asleep with one arm tucked under her head and the other along her side. She had removed her false teeth and her lips and cheeks sucked in a little each time she took a breath. When she exhaled her lips made a little 'pfff' noise.

'Archchi,' Mythil said softly.

'Pfff,' said Archchi. Poor old Archchi was tired. Once before he had tried to wake her up from her afternoon nap and Archchi had found it very difficult to get up. She said it was because all the years she had lived were catching up on her. It would be a shame to wake her, he thought.

Mythil looked at the table by the window. Archchi had been writing a recipe in her notebook. Her pencil and glasses were on the open book. An idea formed in Mythil's mind. He knew he risked getting scolded by his parents if he went through with it but he felt a little reckless.

He reached out for the book through the iron bars careful not to upset Archchi's false teeth, which were in a glass of water. With book and pencil in hand he jumped down and looked at the title of the open page – 'Pumpkin Pudding'. That didn't sound too good. (Mythil only liked chocolate desserts. Anything else, according to him, was suspect.)

Archchi had put down her list of ingredients and had just written down the first step under 'Method – Boil or steam the pumpkin pieces until tender.' Urgh.

Mythil placed the book against the wall and thought for a minute. Then he wrote:

Dear Archchi,
I am runing away but please don't worry.
I will be back by dark.
Don't tell Ammi and Thaththi. Your loving granson
Mythil
PS Irase this after you have read it.

Pleased with his handiwork Mythil pulled himself up to the window again and carefully replaced book and pencil, even remembering to place Archchi's spectacles on top of the book. Then he jumped down and ran full pelt towards the stream, his conscience clear and his sense of adventure kindled.

Who is out there?

Mythil waded across the knee-deep stream carrying his slippers by their rubber thongs. He clambered up the opposite bank and leaned against a slim tree trunk, his heart beating fast as he peered into the jungle. Everything was still and silent. Maybe I should come back tomorrow – in the morning, he thought. Afternoons were notoriously dangerous times to be in a jungle. He looked over his shoulder at the house. It seemed so very far away. He had never seen it at such a distance before.

As he watched, Mythil saw his father storm out of the back door and get into the car. The slam of the car door reached his ears all the way across the stream. Jamis, the gardener ran towards the front garden to open the gate. He saw the car back out jerkily and then disappear around the house at great speed.

Tears pricked the back of Mythil's eyelids. Thaththi had left in a rage – a result of the fight, he was sure. He blinked his tears away. Maybe Thaththi was just going to town to check emails again, he told himself. But the tears persisted. What if his father had got so angry after the fight that he was going away and never coming back? He had heard Thaththi telling Ammi he would do that one day, some months ago when they thought he was asleep.

With a sudden sob Mythil turned blindly and fled into the jungle, running as fast as he could, slapping twigs and branches out of his way. But before he could get very far he stepped on something sharp with his bare feet and groaned to a stop, flinging his slippers to the ground in pain and frustration. A short spray of thorns was stuck to the sole of his foot.

Mythil hobbled to a large stone, sat down, and pulled out the thorns with trembling fingers. He flung it into a bush and squeezed his foot until the thorn puncture bled a little. That way, he thought, remembering a cousin's advice given some years ago, if there's any poison or a broken piece of thorn it will come out rather than travel along my veins and reach my heart. He rubbed his teary eyes and sat for a minute with head on hands. Slowly the heaving in his chest subsided and he became still; as still as the jungle around him.

The silence of the jungle soothed him. He didn't feel afraid. Well, not much anyway. He still kept an eye on anything that moved suddenly. An ash-dove that scurried away into the underbrush. A lizard that shot off down a tree. A faded leaf that dropped from a branch overhead. He looked up at the blue sky through the branches and took a deep breath.

Dead leaves on the jungle floor rustled at the corner of his eye and he turned sharply. A babbler was scratching for worms. Ceylon Rufus Babbler, he proudly identified it to himself. Archchi had shown him a painting of it in her bird book. He often saw these small brown birds in their little garden back in Colombo.

Four more appeared pecking and scratching among the undergrowth. He looked around for the scout sister. Archchi had told him how these 'seven sister' birds always kept a scout on a high branch whenever the others were feeding on the ground. Ah! there she was. She wasn't doing a very good job, Mythil thought. She had found a big caterpillar and was smashing it to pulp against a branch when she should have been keeping a look out.

Mythil began to count the flock again looking for the seventh bird. Before he could finish, the scout sister began to chirp insistently. The danger signal. In a trice the rest of the sisters had taken up the call and flown up into the branches. Mythil looked in the direction they were facing but could see nothing except a thick enclave of trees. He drew his legs up and crouched on top of the stone. He was ready to flee for his life if he caught sight of so much as a wiggle of a serpent's tail.

His heart beat hard against his ribs as he waited. But little by little the distress call waned. The birds began hopping away into the jungle, uttering little chirps as they pecked at the undergrowth. Mythil wished they would stay.

An eerie quiet descended.

Then a twig snapped.

Mythil slipped off the stone stealthily and backed up against a tree. He was careful to face the creeper-covered grove. Then he sidled behind his tree, crouched down and peered out from behind its thick trunk. Snakes did not snap twigs did they? Perhaps a giant snake might. An anaconda or a python? If it's a fat snake maybe I can outrun it without a problem, he thought anxiously.

Were there anacondas and pythons in Sri Lanka? Anacondas? No. They were only found in South America. Pythons? Yes. He remembered Seeli telling him a story about a python. (Seeli knew a lot of scary stories about the jungle.) This story was about a poor man who had gone into the jungle to chop wood. The fallen branch that the poor man had been chopping changed into a giant python and chased him through the forest. Had the snake caught the man? Mythil couldn't remember how the story ended. Maybe fat snakes *could* go faster than humans.

His legs were getting 'pins and needles' so Mythil got slowly on to his feet to give them a chance to get back to normal. Peering around the tree he spotted his slippers near the stone he had sat on. Was it safe to pick them up? He focused on the thicket ahead of him. All was quiet.

Then just as he had decided to reach out for his slippers the hairs on the back of his neck stood up and he felt, rather than heard, something behind him. He turned around sharply flinging himself against the tree.

About five feet away stood an old banyan tree. The tree was enormous and because it stood on a huge rock, it looked as tall as it was wide. Its roots looked like they had melted and poured over the rock before solidifying again. Other roots, which had several feet more to grow before they reached the ground, dangled like ropey beards from thick, dark, leafy branches that blotted out the sky.

But there was no one there. What had scared him, Mythil wondered, his heart still hammering inside him. Two green parakeets flew away from the tree startling him even more, their squawks breaking the silence for a moment. Mythil turned his attention back to the rock. Then he took in a sharp breath. Who was that peering out at him from the rock? In a dark hollow among the giant tree's roots Mythil could make out a grotesque little figure: a grimacing face in a big head, puny little arms and legs around a huge belly.

Then he heaved a sigh of relief. It was just an old rock carving. A carving of a bahirawaya. He remembered Ammi saying something about bahirawayas once. What was it? Ammi had been doing some research for an old professor in campus. According to ancient legends bahirawayas were considered powerful spirits. She had been surprised to learn that in some parts of the country, many centuries before; even human sacrifices had been made to them. Mythil shuddered.

A twig snapped again and he froze. Something or someone was out there and it was *definitely* bigger than a seven sister bird. Definitely bigger. Did pythons live in tree hollows? He felt like kicking himself. He watched so many nature programmes on TV but he couldn't remember where they said pythons lived. The bahirawaya's tree had many hollows and he noticed several charred, clay lamps at the foot of the rock.

Mythil sidled around the trunk of his tree so that he could keep an eye on both the thicket and the banyan tree. He knew he was in full sight of both but that couldn't be helped.

Thankfully the gloomy green undergrowth and the creepy roots stayed still. He flicked his eyes in the direction of the banyan tree and noticed bunches of dead flowers among the charred lamps. Someone still visited the bahirawaya. Could it be poachers?

Perhaps not. He found it difficult to imagine that ruthless poachers would fear a tiny bahirawaya. In his mind's eye the poachers wore gold earrings and eye-patches, looking very much like the pirates in his illustrated story books. It was unlikely that such a rowdy bunch would leave flowers at the foot of a revered old tree. If there really *were* poachers in the jungle, he thought practically. The village was nearby. Perhaps people still visited this rough old shrine.

The jungle remained silent, but the feeling that someone was watching him increased.

Something stung his ear and he jumped, rubbing his earlobe. Was someone throwing stones at him? Whatever had struck his left ear must have been quite small because he couldn't see it on the ground. Who was out there?

Mythil couldn't bear it. 'Who's there?' he called out. Even though he told himself that there were no poachers his voice still came out all shaky.

'Come out and show yourself,' he said trying to make his voice sound steadier, 'Come out! Do you hear me? I want to see you.'

Silence.

Then he caught a movement above his head. With a gasp he spun away from the tree and looked up into its branches. Perched on the fork of a branch overhead, crouched and ready to spring was a … was a … what was it? Matted and tangled hair framed a dark grimy face, bared teeth and bulgy eyes.

'Yaka!' Mythil was screaming but the words came out in a hoarse whisper. For what seemed like forever he could only stand there petrified. In slow motion he saw the horrifying creature spring off the branch towards him. The next thing Mythil knew he was tearing through the underbrush, his entire being focused on getting out of that jungle. He leapt over rocks and broke through thickets with uncanny speed. He was moving faster than any of his computer game characters, but to his speeding mind his movements seemed sluggish and slow. Would he reach the stream before the creature caught him?

Scary stories

Gasping for breath and dripping with sweat Mythil broke out of the jungle and splashed across the stream. He turned and frantically scanned the trees with terrified eyes. Fear propelled him towards the house.

Seeli was by the kitchen door deftly flipping drying grains of kurakkan in a reed kulla. Mythil flung himself on the grass in front of her looking behind him to see if the yaka had followed him to the house.

'Where have you been wandering Podi Baby?' Seeli asked, her eyes on the kulla. She picked out an odd grain of barley from among the grains of kurakkan and popped it into her mouth.

'Seeli, I was in the jungle. I saw a yaka.' Mythil could see the grain of barley glistening on her tongue as she stared at him open mouthed.

'Podi Baby! What happened?' Seeli's voice had risen dramatically.

'In the jungle, on a tree, I saw a yaka,' Mythil said again trying to breathe evenly.

'Aiyo! What were you doing in the jungle at this time Podi Baby! Don't you know that it isn't safe? Why even I don't go into the jungle without an iron nail tied around my neck.' She lowered her voice to a whisper, glancing over his shoulder at the garden. 'You have to carry iron with you, you know, and the spirits can't touch you. Did this one do anything to you?'

Mythil shook his head, his lips and body trembling.

Then Archchi appeared in the doorway with Ammi behind her. 'What happened?' Archchi asked sharply. Mythil ran up the steps to the pantry and flung his arms around her. He was so overcome with relief that he couldn't speak. So Seeli left her perch on the kitchen step and told Archchi how Mythil had almost been attacked by a tree-spirit.

'A yaka?' Archchi said, 'So you ran away to the jungle and saw yakas?' and to Mythil's relief she began laughing.

'You ran away Mythil?' Ammi asked scornfully. Her eyes were red and

Mythil could see the frown lines on her forehead. 'Running away never solves anything,' she said bitterly and Mythil knew she was talking about Thaththi.

'You sit down with me and tell me all about the yaka you saw, will you,' Archchi told Mythil with one of her sunny smiles.

'Don't laugh Loku Nona,' Seeli said. 'And don't call the spirits by their name – they can hear! The jungle is full of them. Especially at this time. And Podi Baby was eating kevili – I saw. You must always drink some water after eating kevili in the afternoon – especially if you're going outside. Yakas are attracted to the smell of kevili . . .'

'That's enough Seeli,' Archchi said sternly. 'Don't scare Podi Baby.' Seeli pursed her lips in a thin, obstinate line. 'It's true what I said,' she sniffed, flicking the kurakkan with a 'sruss' sound and grinding the grain of barley between her teeth as she walked away.

'Now don't listen to her nonsense,' Archchi said lifting Mythil's chin with her hand. 'Tell me what happened.'

So they sat down on the pantry steps and Mythil began to tell his grandmother what he had seen. One of Archchi's cats crept on to her lap with a wary eye on Mythil. It was soon purring contentedly and listening to Mythil's story with Archchi. Ammi stood behind them leaning against the lintel.

'How big was he?' Archchi asked about the yaka. Mythil forced his mind to re-conjure the image he had seen.

'Not very big Archchi,' he said. 'Maybe my size.'

'Then shall I tell you what you saw?' Archchi said with a comforting chuckle. 'I'm sure you saw one of the village boys playing in the jungle. He would have seen you and thought of frightening you a little for fun.'

Ammi turned away and went back into the house without saying anything.

'So you don't think I saw a yaka Archchi?' Mythil asked hopefully. He felt his earlobe gingerly. It still stung from whatever had struck it in the jungle. Perhaps Archchi was right. Yakas wouldn't throw stones at people, would they? But a boy might.

Archchi laughed again. 'I'm sure it's just a village boy. Next time you see him tell him to stop scaring you or that old Jamis will beat him black and blue. Or tell him to come and have some rice if he is hungry. Then you will have someone your age to play with at least.'

'At first I was scared it was a snake,' Mythil told Archchi reaching out to pet the purring cat which now had its eyes tightly shut in feline contentment. He was eager to prove to his grandmother that he hadn't been completely fooled by the village boy. 'It could have been a poacher too couldn't it Archchi? Or a robber with grease on his face – planning to steal from a house?'

'Ah, that reminds me, have I ever told you the story of how I chased a robber?' Archchi asked.

'You chased a robber Archchi? On your own?' The cat opened its eyes and leapt off Archchi's lap with a hiss. It had just realised that Mythil was petting it. Archchi took no notice.

'Yes. Your Seeya was still alive then.' Archchi's eyes misted over as they always did when she spoke of her husband. He had died of a heart attack when Mythil's mother was still a young girl and Archchi had brought up her three children on her own.

She began her story. 'Seeya had taken Jamis to his hometown in the car and hadn't yet returned,' Archchi said. 'It was past midnight and I was waiting up till Seeya came back.' Mythil rested his head on Archchi's shoulder picturing her patiently sitting in the hall till his grandfather returned.

'The house was in darkness. There was just one lamp lit in the front veranda. Then I saw a shadow moving in the garden.'

'Like from the corner of your eye?' Mythil asked. 'Like you weren't sure you saw something but you had to turn your head to see? That's just how I saw the yaka... I mean the village boy.'

'Yes, just like that,' Archchi said. 'Your Ammi and her brothers were sleeping in their bedrooms. Seeli was in the kitchen. I knew it couldn't be any of them. The person moved closer to the veranda entrance. When the lamplight fell on him I saw that it was a man with grease on his body. I knew at once it was a rogue then. I had heard they applied grease so that it would be difficult to catch and grab hold of them.' Mythil shivered deliciously.

'I slowly took down your grandfather's gun from where it used to hang in the hall. Then I walked out onto the veranda and pointed it at the man. I said, "Who's there?"'

Archchi held out her hands as if she was holding an imaginary gun and said the words with force and menace. Her mouth was set in a firm line and her eyes shone fiercely. Mythil could imagine how scary she must have looked in the shadows made by the lamplight.

'The man jumped,' Archchi said, continuing her story. 'He hadn't expected anyone to be awake. In those days, before we got electricity to the house, we usually went to sleep soon after it got dark.'

'Were you scared Archchi?' Mythil asked, putting his arm around her waist.

'My hands were trembling,' Archchi admitted. 'And I knew the gun had no bullets.'

'No bullets!' Mythil asked in horror. Archchi had had no real defence!

'No, with the children around your Seeya never kept a loaded gun in the house. So I had to be very stern. I asked, "Who are you man? Can you see this gun?" and the man began to stammer. So I knew he was scared. And I said, "If you want to live run away from here. Run away!" and he ran.'

'He got scared!' Mythil crowed clapping his hands together in delight. 'Archchi you are *so* brave.'

Archchi laughed. 'Now wash your face and come and have your tea,' she said getting up from the step with a little difficulty. Mythil put his arm around her to support her. She smiled at him and gently patted his cheek. 'You can help me make pumpkin pudding.'

She went inside to make the tea followed by the mewing cat and Mythil went to the half-filled bucket that stood by the well to have his wash. Seeli came and poured fresh water for him after he had soaped himself.

'All I am saying,' she told him in a low voice and with a glance at the pantry windows, 'is don't go into the jungle without a piece of iron. And don't call them by their real name – they are jungle spirits and when you say their name they are drawn to you.'

'But what do they do?' Mythil asked washing his feet. Until that afternoon he hadn't really believed in yakas.

Seeli sloshed water into the kalaya, and spoke from the corner of her mouth. 'They possess you so that they can become more powerful,' she said hefting the kalaya on to her hip. Then looking over her shoulder as though she expected to see a troupe of yakas waiting to pounce on her, she hurried towards the kitchen.

Waking up

It was while Archchi was chopping up slices of wattakka that they heard Thaththi's car drive in. But Mythil pretended not to hear. He wished he could forget about his parents. It was so much more peaceful being with Archchi. He picked up a cinnamon stick, breathing in its fragrance. Using it like a mini cricket bat he flicked the nutmeg around the table.

'Urgh, Archchi, why are you cutting up wattakka?' he asked.

'To make pumpkin pudding, of course,' Archchi said checking her recipe book to make sure she had all the ingredients.

'So where is the pumpkin?' Mythil asked, looking for the perfect round, orange pumpkin of his storybooks.

Archchi laughed. 'Wattakka is a type of pumpkin, you silly-billy!' Silly-billy was a word Archchi had picked up from Mythil's Colombo cousins. 'Pumpkin is the English name.'

'Ahhh,' Mythil said nodding wisely as he made the connection for the first time. He watched Archchi place the wattakka slices on a plate leaving only one on the chopping board.

'So, if you think about it, Cinderella's fairy godmother changed one of these wattakkas into a coach, no?' he said. 'Wow!' They laughed together drowning out the low buzz of angry, insistent voices from his parents' bedroom.

'Why isn't it round and orange like it is in the storybooks?' Mythil asked tapping the thick rubbery skin of the wattakka.

'Why? Isn't this pretty enough for you?' Archchi asked, nudging his hand out of the way and deftly slicing the wattakka. She picked up a slice from the plate and showed him the glossy, green streaked beige skin. 'Look at that! It's like the grain you get on wood, and it's glossy and smooth! Wouldn't you like to have a car painted like this?'

Mythil frowned as he tried to imagine a beige car covered in green veins. Spooky!

'Here, now remember this is how you choose a good pumpkin,' Archchi said pointing to the wattakka flesh nearest to the skin. 'Always make sure that this area is a nice, healthy green. Then you know the pumpkin is fresh. Learn that so that when you bring home the vegetables your wife will be proud of you,' she said with a twinkle in her eye.

Mythil blushed. 'Aiyo Archchi! Don't be silly,' he protested, 'I'm never ever going to get married!' The two of them giggled together.

'Anay, then you won't have anyone to make you wattakka pudding no?' Archchi teased. 'Here, you better watch and learn how to make it on your own then.'

'Mythil.'

Archchi and Mythil both looked up. Thaththi stood in the doorway. 'Mythil, get into the car,' he said in a low voice.

'Where are we going?' Mythil asked in surprise.

His father didn't reply.

Mythil looked at Archchi. She had an awful look on her face. 'Now putha . . .' she said gently to her son-in-law, her voice shaking a little. She looked old and tired. Gone was the gleam of the robber-chaser, the triumph of the demon-disbeliever. In their place stood fear and despair.

Mythil felt scared. Was Thaththi going to take him away with him and never come back again? Was that why Archchi looked so upset? 'I don't want to leave Archchi!' he wailed at his father. He didn't want her to look so lost and old. He wanted to hug her and tell her that everything would be okay.

But his legs wouldn't move. And his jaws locked. And his father thundered at him to get into the car. And so Mythil went.

He heard Thaththi and Archchi speaking in low voices. He heard Ammi crying in her room. He got into the car and banged the door shut. If he could only shut out the world, he thought.

Thaththi got in and started the car. He didn't speak. Mythil had drawn his legs up on the seat, folded his arms across his knees and put his head down. He heard the engine turn and felt the car begin to move. Still he remained motionless. The car sped along the gravel lane towards the main road.

Gradually, exhaustion and the soothing motion of the car lulled him to sleep. He did not wake when his father stopped the car and put his seat belt on him. He did not wake when they reached journey's end. Mythil slept on, dreaming troubled dreams of yakas and pythons and other faceless, nameless terrors.

The next morning as soon as he woke up, the events of the past day screamed through Mythil's mind, scattering sleep in a rush. With his eyes still shut he remembered his parents fight, his encounter with the yaka and then Thaththi appearing in the pantry and ordering him into the car. The rest of his memories were vague. He remembered stumbling upstairs, supported by his father, washing his feet, removing his T-shirt and at last lying down with his head on something soft and comfortable. He remembered in snatches hushed voices speaking on and on into the night. But nothing more.

Slowly, Mythil rubbed his eyes clear and then opened them. He was in someone's hall. On a rattan settee. Although the curtains were drawn a sky-light let in a few faint sunbeams. It felt like early morning. He looked around him. The room was small and had white walls which were hung over with red pennants that had gold-embroidered Chinese characters on them. The furniture was wood and cane with fat, red, velvet cushions on them. Other doorways could be seen leading out of the hall. It reminded him of a dolls house one of the girls in his school van had brought a term ago.

Mythil sat up cautiously. No one else seemed to be around. He was rubbing at the rattan imprint on his arm when something caught his attention. Peeping out from under one of the fat red cushions he noticed a 'neek-neek' game (that's what he and his cousins called the Game Boy consoles that had been carefully handed down from eldest to youngest). Mythil picked it up eagerly. He was sure it was a new PlayStation Portable.

Mythil knew that the PSP had several games built into one machine so it was much better than a Game Boy. He'd only ever played on a PSP once for a few minutes when one of his classmates had brought it to school on the sly. They had had to be careful not to get caught by a teacher or prefect and have the game confiscated.

He switched it on with trembling fingers but was disappointed – nothing happened. Just his luck, he thought bitterly. He'd been wishing for his own neek-neek game for his last birthday but he'd had no luck with that either. He knew his parents couldn't afford it.

He looked around for a toilet. Several doorways opened into the hall. Through the bead curtain of one of them he saw what looked like the dining room. Somewhere towards the back of the house he could hear the clink of dishes and pans. Someone was up but they were trying to be very quiet.

He tiptoed over to a doorway on his left and heard snoring. Peeping in on the snorer, Mythil wasn't surprised to see his father on a narrow bed in a tiny room. It looked like a girl's room. Almost everything was pink – the work table and desk lamp, the bed sheet and pillow case, the mosquito net which his father hadn't bothered to use, the curtains and the fluffy rug by the bed. A closed door looked promising and he was lucky. He had found the toilet.

When he came out, the house seemed still to be asleep. His father snored on. In the hall he couldn't hear any sounds from the kitchen either. Had whoever it was, gone back to bed? Should he wake Thaththi, he wondered, looking back at his sleeping father. Why had Thaththi brought him here? Had they run away from Ammi and Archchi?

Mythil felt sick at the thought of how worried Archchi and Ammi must be. If he had really run away to the jungle for the night he knew that Thaththi and Ammi would have scolded him for making them worry. But last night, he felt sure, Thaththi had taken him away from Ammi to get even with her for starting the fight. Even Archchi knew that – that's why she had asked Thaththi not to take him away. When will I *ever* understand grown-ups, Mythil wondered contemptuously. They were always on at you to grow up but then look at the way *they* behaved.

A window looked out over an empty and sleepy back street. He was surprised to see that he was one storey up. Then he remembered staggering upstairs the previous night. He tiptoed back into the hall and noticed a narrow wooden stairway. It led down to the ground floor. The storey below was dark but a sliver of daylight showed that a door leading out had been opened. Mythil decided to explore.

One of them

The stairs creaked a little as he climbed down. He paused on the last step and his stomach growled in the silence. He was in a room that was cluttered with racks and tables filled with odds and ends. It took him a while to realise where he was. The stairs had led to the back of a darkened shop full of the strangest knick-knacks.

Mythil looked around with interest. His eyes were drawn to a cabinet that was chock-a-block with curious green ornaments. He peered through glass doors, fascinated by the objects inside. An emerald glass cat. A jade dragon. Intricately carved ornaments made of a mouldy green metal – vases, an old ink pot, trinket boxes and various bits and pieces. In a dark corner – what was it – a green glass yaka?

A pale face appeared above his shoulder in the reflection of the cabinet's glass doors and Mythil jumped aside, nearly upsetting another rack of oddments. An old woman glared at him.

'Don't touch the glass. It will get dirty,' she told him irritably. Then she moved away towards the half-open doorway of the shop. A smouldering incense-holder lay on a folded newspaper on one of the glass counters. She held a white handkerchief to her nose and put a pinch of powder into the holder. Sweet smelling smoke billowed from the shell-shaped holder and collected like a cloud under the ceiling. She held the handle with another handkerchief and sent the smoke around the shop carefully, making sure that every corner received a generous share.

Mythil wondered whether she was the PSP owner's grandmother. He watched her carefully moving the incense-holder around. This was something he had always wanted to try out. 'Can I do that?' Mythil asked her.

She gave an amused smile and beckoned to him, tucking one of her handkerchiefs into the waistband of her grey and white saree but keeping the other in front of her nose. Mythil tested the iron holder with his finger.

It wasn't hot, so he picked it up. She moved his arm in circles to show him how to distribute the sweet-smelling smoke evenly. Her fingers felt cold against his wrist. Mythil moved slowly towards the door under her watchful eyes. He waved the holder carefully as he had been directed. When he reached the entrance he wondered what to do.

'Outside,' the woman motioned to him flapping her hands outwards. On the street Mythil saw other shopkeepers letting incense fumes waft around their shops. A boy a little older than himself was sprinkling the pavement opposite with yellow, turmeric water out of an old plastic bottle. Mythil felt awkward. He was bare-bodied and bare-footed and felt embarrassed to be out in public like that – like a street urchin, Ammi would have said. He felt a pang of homesickness as he thought of his mother.

But the old lady had stepped out and now stood on the pavement impatiently. 'Soon, soon,' she said. Mythil half-heartedly swung the incense-holder on either side of the entrance and turned to go back in. But the old woman was in the way. The smoke wafted away from waist-height – up and over the roof-tops.

'Do it properly!' the old woman ordered still standing at the entrance. 'You know why it is important to do it properly, no?' Mythil looked at his toes. He didn't like the scolding voice she was using. It wasn't fair for her to order him about, he thought. After all, he was doing her a favour, wasn't he?

'We are doing this to keep the evil ones away,' she said with her hands on her hips. Mythil sent the smoke wafting towards the awning of the shop trying not to look self-conscious. The old lady kept talking.

'So is that enough when you just swing the smoke around? What if there was one hiding? Like this?' She suddenly squatted under the wafting smoke and for a split second, her face turned green – like the green yaka thing on the shelf inside. And her eyes smouldered like the coals in the incense-holder.

Mythil gasped and stepped back. In moments the yaka face had transformed back again and the old woman stood up slowly, narrowed iron-grey eyes looking at him shrewdly. 'What is it?' she asked, not taking her eyes off him. She took a step towards Mythil one hand reaching for his shoulder. 'What did you see?' she asked in a hoarse whisper.

He tried to say 'Yaka,' but the words stuck in his throat. His feet were rooted to the spot. Where could he run? Nowhere. She was blocking the door that led to his father. And he didn't have an iron nail on him.

Iron! He looked down at the incense holder. It was iron. He held it up in front of her face and she stepped back. But the smoke was lessening and her piercing eyes bored into his. 'What did you see?' she asked again, compelling him to answer her.

It was a weird feeling. He felt awed by her power. He had to fight a feeling of lifelessness and his hand shook and his fingers threatened to slip on the handle. He pushed towards her but though she evaded the incense holder, she did not take a step back. Just one step back and he would have had access to the door.

It felt like the concrete of the pavement had liquefied and then hardened around his ankles. Mythil stole a lightning glance at the boy with the bottle of yellow water. He had finished his job and was going back inside. People passing by on the street didn't give him a second look. No one seemed to have noticed that there was a yaka on the street.

Then Thaththi stood in the doorway. The incense holder clattered to the pavement as Mythil flung himself against his father. Thaththi managed to keep his balance, and Mythil didn't care that everyone was looking then. The mudalali dusting his shop's counter. A man on a bicycle passing by. The boy with the empty yellow-water bottle, who had reappeared with a soggy broom. A woman chewing betel. Mythil buried his sweaty face against his father's waist, blocking out all of them.

'Mythil! You spilt the incense,' he heard his father say reproachfully. But Mythil clung on like a limpet. Then he heard the old woman speak. 'Never mind, I think the boy is not very well. Fever or something.' His father tried to look at his face but Mythil clung even tighter. 'Good if you take him inside,' she said, in her sandpapery voice.

Mythil lifted his head and peered over his father's shoulder as Thaththi half-carried him inside. The old woman was squatting by the ashes on the pavement but she was looking directly at him.

'Mythil, what is it?' his father asked as he supported Mythil up the stairs. 'You're sweating! Have you got fever?' He felt his father's hand on his forehead. 'She's a ... she's one of them ...' he mumbled his words slurring. And then the white walls and red pennants of the room began to whirl faster and faster around them. Everything blurred.

Where are we?

Mythil concentrated on a single red pennant and thankfully watched it slow down. He heard his father's troubled voice. He heard a soft female voice and then another low male voice. He heard bits of conversation that didn't make sense to him. Unrelated phrases with big, meaningless words like 'traumatic experience,' 'parents must be tolerant,' 'marriage counselling,' and 'irreparable psychological damage'.

And then, quite clearly, he heard the female voice say, gently: 'It's always the children who suffer. For his sake, you should try to make things work out.' And then there was silence.

Mythil sat up. Thaththi's arm steadied him. 'Take it slowly Mythie-boy. How are you feeling?' he asked very gently . . . Mythil blinked around at the room which had got much brighter now that the curtains had been drawn aside. Opposite them sat a middle-aged couple. The woman had her hair piled elegantly on top of her head and she wore a red and yellow floral dress. The man wore a blue sarong and grey t-shirt. He looked Chinese.

A girl about his age was peeping at him from behind the bead curtain. As soon as Mythil looked at her she turned with a swish of her white nightie and the beads in the curtain clicked and swayed together. The woman sat on the edge of her chair. In her hands she held a blue and white china bowl with a ceramic spoon and some soup in it.

'No wonder you fainted! You haven't had any dinner!' she told Mythil, smiling warmly. 'Will you have some soup? It will make you feel much better,' she added coaxingly. Mythil's tummy growled in answer. He certainly felt hungry.

'Thanks Nilmini,' Thaththi said reaching out for the bowl. He brought a spoonful of soup to Mythil's lips. Despite having bits of carrots and some green things floating around in it the soup smelt very good so Mythil slurped some of it into his mouth. Delicious. He took the bowl and spoon from his father.

'I'm sorry to have barged in on you like this last night,' Thaththi was saying. Things just came to a head last evening. It's so disappointing to check email everyday and never hear anything positive. I can't remember how many job applications I've sent out now. Sometimes it just gets to me. You've both been very helpful.'

Mythil was only half listening. The china spoon was awkward to use but he was so hungry that the soup was disappearing fast, vegetables and all.

'We're very happy to help,' Aunty Nilmini said. 'Anthony knows the editor in Hong Kong very well. He'll put in a word. The main thing is to make sure that they see your application – you've plenty of experience and published work to show.' She looked at her husband who nodded in agreement.

'Don't lose hope,' Aunty Nilmini went on. 'And for the sake of the child . . .' she broke off and Thaththi nodded.

Sensing that they were all looking at him, Mythil looked up from his soup. He wanted to ask them about the yaka downstairs but suddenly he felt shy. What if, like the people on the street, they didn't know she was a yaka? He turned to Thaththi instead.

'Where are we?' Mythil asked.

'We are at a friend's house,' Thaththi said. 'Uncle Anthony is a lawyer. Aunty Nilmini keeps the shop downstairs. They used to live in China.'

'In Hong Kong actually,' Uncle Anthony said smiling and rubbing his greying hair.

Thaththi apologised for the error as Mythil gulped: 'And. . . downstairs. . . ?'

Aunty Nilmini answered, 'That's Aunty Bhishani. She is an old friend of ours.' Then she turned to Mythil's father.

'Actually Bhishani's the one who runs the shop now. These days I'm quite busy with my counselling work so she runs it on her own. She used to have her own antique shop a long time ago, so she is very clever when it comes to running a business.'

Aunty Nilmini smiled at Mythil. 'I'm sure she is very worried about you too.'

Mythil turned to Thaththi. 'I want to go home,' he said in a low voice. He knew it was rude to say so in front of their hosts but he couldn't help it. The whole experience had been too much for him and he wanted the comfort of known places and people.

'Yes, it is time we went,' Thaththi said much to Mythil's relief. 'I want to leave before the office rush.' He helped his son into his t-shirt.

'Would you like to wait here till I bring the car around?' Thaththi asked Mythil.

Mythil shook his head. He felt angry at his father for forcing him to be rude again. Hadn't he just told Thaththi that he wanted to go home? Why would he want to stay alone in the home of a yaka a minute longer? Obviously Aunty Nilmini and Uncle Anthony had no idea that the old woman was a demon.

Soon they were saying their thank yous and good byes and were making their way downstairs. The shop still smelt of incense and Mythil clung tightly to Thaththi's hand. But the old woman was not to be seen. The pavement outside had been swept clean of ashes.

They were almost at the door when Thaththi stopped. 'Actually I think I should just call Ammi and tell her we'll be home by lunch time,' he told Mythil taking his mobile phone out. Mythil's heart sank. Another delay!

'Oh no! My battery's dead,' Thaththi said looking at his phone in dismay.

'Oh you can use our phone,' Aunty Nilmini said. She still had the soup bowl in her hand.

'Yes, we insist,' Uncle Anthony said, leading Thaththi back up stairs.

Aunty Nilmini handed the bowl of soup to Mythil. 'Why don't you finish it?' she asked sitting on a step.

Mythil spooned the rest of the soup into his mouth mechanically. He wasn't hungry any more but he couldn't think of anything to say to this strange lady with her bright smile and staring eyes.

'Is this the first time you fainted Mythil?' Aunty Nilmini asked and Mythil nodded looking around the shop again to avoid her gaze. 'Fainting can be quite scary!' Aunty Nilmini went on. 'I remember when I first fainted

– what felt the strangest was not being able to remember one minute of my life. I was playing hide and seek as a child and I got into a huge iron pot to hide and the next minute I was being carried out by my friend's parents all shivery and shaky. I couldn't remember a thing!' She shuddered and then smiled again.

But Mythil couldn't smile back. A horrid thought had just struck him. She had fainted in an iron pot. Could she be a yaka too? No, he hadn't seen her eyes glow. You're being silly, he told himself. But that didn't stop him from looking around for the iron incense-holder. It was nowhere to be seen. He slowly placed the soup bowl on a counter and edged away pretending to look at the ornaments.

'Can I get you some more?' Aunty Nilmini asked. Mythil shook his head staring at her eyes to see if they glowed. Aunty Nilmini smiled at him, picked up the bowl and went inside as her husband appeared at the top of the steps.

Uncle Anthony stood awkwardly for a minute as though wondering whether to come down and talk to Mythil or follow his wife inside. 'Are you feeling better?' he asked at last. Mythil nodded. 'Good, good,' Uncle Anthony said nodding his head and smiling uncomfortably.

Mythil looked out through the half open door at the pavement. It seemed to have got quite busy outside. He could see people walking past on their way to work. A little boy tried to peer in at the dark shop interior as he walked past with his mother but she dragged him on. When Mythil looked back at the top of the stairs Uncle Anthony had disappeared.

Mythil was alone in the shop once more. This time his eyes rested on the yaka trinket in the glass cabinet. He opened the door a crack, picked up the ornament and closed the door again. It looked uncannily like the yaka face of the old woman, he thought. As the memory of that face flashed in his mind the trinket slipped from his fingers and clattered under the cabinet. He crouched down and scrabbled around for it until his fingers closed around the cold little glass ornament. It fitted neatly in his hand.

Still sitting on his heels, Mythil looked at the trinket to make sure it was not damaged. He shook it and something made a clinking noise inside. 'Oh no – it must be broken!' Mythil thought in dismay.

From above he could hear adult voices coming closer to the stairway.

'It's really nice of you to arrange this visit at such short notice,' Thaththi was saying.

'Not at all,' Uncle Anthony said. 'We do our best for the children.'

'I hope it won't affect your work,' Thaththi said.

'No, no. It's time I took a day off to spend with the family. I haven't done that at all this holiday,' Uncle Anthony said.

'And it's a nice drive . . .' Aunty Nilmini was saying.

Their voices drifted down from the hall above but Mythil wasn't paying much attention to what was being said. He was looking at the ornament. It looked eerie in the dim light. If anyone asks me what the old woman's yaka face looks like I can always point to this ornament, he thought.

And then another thought struck him. What if the old woman comes and takes it away after we leave? She knows now that I saw her real face. What if she breaks it – I'll never see it again. Perhaps he could get Thaththi to buy it for him? He checked the price tag. Wow! He breathed out through pursed lips. Way too expensive. Thaththi would never agree.

He was about to get up and put the ornament back in the cabinet when someone came bounding down the steps. Quick as a flash Mythil slipped the green, glass trinket in to his pocket and stood up.

It was the girl he had seen earlier. She was in a pair of pink shorts and a matching Hello Kitty t-shirt now. Her short hair was pushed back from her face by a pink band. Mythil was conscious again that his own hair was tousled and his feet were bare.

'Oh, hello!' she said surprised by Mythil's sudden appearance. 'Were you hiding?'

'No,' Mythil said shortly. He was always shy around other kids and that sometimes made him appear unfriendly. Even in school, although he was never the last one to be picked for a game of cricket or football, he didn't have any close friends and was a bit of a loner.

'Did you come very late last night?' she went on. 'I got quite a shock to wake up and find you and your dad here in the morning. Your dad slept in my room didn't he?'

Mythil nodded.

'My dad must have carried me into their room in the night and I never even woke up! Did you sleep on the sofa? That would've been too small for your dad to sleep on, wouldn't it?' Mythil shrugged, looking towards the stairway and wishing his father would hurry up. Almost on cue Thaththi appeared at the top of the steps.

'There you are Mythil,' Thaththi said. 'Ready to go?'

Mythil nodded. Of course he was ready. That's all he had wanted to do since waking up that morning – leave these strangers and go back to Archchi's.

Thaththi smiled and said hello to the girl as he walked past her. She grinned back at him in a friendly way and Mythil envied her confidence.

Uncle Anthony and Aunty Nilmini came down into the shop waving goodbye. Mythil and his father waved back and set off down the pavement.

No such thing as monsters

'Where are your slippers?' Thaththi asked Mythil as they walked along the pavement. 'You look a proper little scallywag.' But Mythil had detected the playful note in his voice as Thaththi ruffled his hair so he paid no attention.

Instead Mythil looked around at the bustling street. Office girls clip-clopped past in high heels with handbags under their arms. A road sweeper pushed a hand cart along collecting the neat piles of swept up rubbish at the edges of the pavement. The only inactive living thing was a dog fast asleep on the side of the road.

As they neared a junction he noticed a group of people gathered around a newspaper seller who doubled as a fruit merchant. The man was calling out, 'Annasi, amba, kolikuttu, diwul!' to people. He only stopped to say something sharp to an old man who took too long to pay for a comb of plantains.

'All right, all right,' he heard the old fellow say. 'I'm not going to run away with your fruit without paying.'

Mythil's heart beat fast at the thought of being found with the trinket in his pocket. I'm just borrowing it he told himself, but it was no use. He knew that wasn't true. He had stolen from a shop. He'd never done anything like that before. Should he confess to Thaththi?

But that would mean going back and perhaps meeting the yaka woman. Maybe he should just drop the ornament on the road, he thought. Putting his hand in his pocket he half pulled it out. But what if someone saw me drop it and came running after us and gave it back, he thought. Thaththi would ask all kinds of awkward questions about it – especially when he saw the price tag. Mythil's shoulders drooped as he let the ornament drop back into his pocket.

'Come on Mythil. Don't be such a slow coach,' Thaththi said a little impatiently and Mythil hurried to catch up. He caught sight of an old woman buying newspapers and fruit and craned his neck to see if it was the yaka-lady. No, she was an ordinary old woman.

He scanned the faces in the crowd and quite suddenly the fruit seller looked straight at him – *with the face of a yaka!* He had glowing red eyes and tiny tusks protruding from under his upper lip. Mythil gasped. They had reached a corner and by then the newspaper/fruit seller disappeared from sight along with his buyers.

He kept turning his head back until Thaththi stopped impatiently. 'What is it?' Thaththi asked. 'Did you forget something?'

Mythil shook his head, tugging at his father's shirt to make him go on. He took a last look at the corner as they got into the car. Thaththi pulled out of the parking space and set off homeward. No yaka followed them. No one stared at them. From where he sat, with his head out of the window, the street looked like any other street. The people looked normal.

'Do you want to tell me what happened this morning at the shop?' Thaththi asked conversationally as they turned on to the long road that led to Archchi's.

'That old woman,' Mythil said turning away from the window, 'She was a . . . tree spirit.' Mythil was a little puzzled as to what kind of spirit the old woman was – there had been no trees in the vicinity. He decided not to tell Thaththi about the fruit seller. He *had* to have seen wrong about that – that must have been his imagination.

Thaththi went all quiet for a bit and Mythil wondered whether he was losing his temper again. 'What did she do?' Thaththi asked at last. Mythil was relieved that he didn't sound impatient. He relived those awful minutes alone with the yaka.

'She didn't think I would see. Nobody else saw. But she turned into a yaka. Just her face. And when she knew I saw, she got . . .' Mythil searched for the word, 'She got fierce.'

'Did she try to hit you?' Thaththi asked in a concerned voice.

'No, she just looked fierce and said, "What did you see?"' Mythil said imitating the old woman's threatening tones.

'Why did she ask that? What *did* you see?' Thaththi asked sounding puzzled.

Mythil shrugged. 'It was like a door opened in my head and I saw her real face. It was green, like the yaka in the glass cupboard,' Mythil bit his lip and his hand automatically slipped into his pocket again. 'And . . . and she had big red glowing eyes. And her teeth were like a skeleton's teeth.' He frowned at that, putting his fingers to his own mouth. 'She didn't have lips!' he realised. 'And she had long fangs.'

Thaththi kept his eyes on the road sounding the horn impatiently as a three-wheeler driver cut in front of them without signalling. Oh-oh, he's losing his temper again, Mythil thought.

Thaththi certainly did look like he was about to say something sharp to Mythil but then changed his mind. He waited till a man with a handcart crossed the road before putting the car in gear and driving on.

At last he spoke. 'Mythil, you were upset and you hadn't had any dinner – I don't think you were seeing right. There are no such things as monsters or aliens or whatever you thought you saw,' Thaththi said. 'You're old enough to know that.'

Mythil sighed. Thaththi didn't believe him and he couldn't use the ornament to show what the yaka looked like because he'd stolen it. Perhaps Thaththi was right. Both times when he saw the spirits he was upset. Perhaps his mind was playing tricks on him.

Well, he was upset because Ammi and Thaththi were fighting. If they stopped fighting perhaps the yakas would go away. He wished he could say that to Thaththi but he didn't want any unpleasantness. He just wanted them all to get along. So he swallowed what he wanted to say.

Instead, Mythil looked out of the window blinking back tears of frustration. His head hurt. He worried about his parents. He worried about the yakas. And now he worried about the ornament he had stolen. It seemed to be burning a hole in his pocket but he knew that was just guilt.

Think about something else, he told himself looking out at the trees and rows of shops they were driving past. They were now in the suburbs of Colombo and the pavements were crowded with people. The rush hour had started and oncoming traffic was at a standstill. Their lane was fairly empty of course because they were heading away from the city and he and

Thaththi were able to sail through. They would soon be back at Archchi's he thought and felt a little happier.

He rolled up the window on his side as they sped along, wondering how Archchi and Ammi were. Had Archchi made the pumpkin pudding after all, he wondered. Seeli was sure to have helped. Ammi would have been too angry and upset to have done anything normal like cooking.

He sighed when he thought about how angry his parents could sometimes get. There. He was thinking about them again. Something else, something else ... He thought gratefully of Seeli. If she hadn't told him that yakas were afraid of iron he wouldn't have known how to defend himself against the yaka in the shop. He thought about the yaka in the jungle. Was it as powerful as the shop yaka? It seemed a lot smaller.

Mythil rubbed his bare feet on the rubber car mat. They felt grimy. Dare he go back into the jungle alone to get back his slippers? What would happen if the yaka followed him back to the house? Would iron stop it?

He shivered as he pictured hoards of yakas swarming into Archchi's house through those big windows. What if he was the only one who could see the yakas even then? And what if nobody else believed him when he said the house was full of them?

After about three quarters of an hour imagining horrible scenes like that Mythil realised that they were slowing down. They had been driving through a sleepy little town. Now Thaththi was parking their blue car next to a small box of a shop with a telephone sign over it and the word 'Communications'.

'I'll just check my emails, okay?' Thaththi said. 'I haven't checked mail since yesterday. Wouldn't want to miss any new assignments if they came along. Will you be all right alone in the car?'

Mythil nodded, winding down the shutter completely. The smell of freshly baked bread wafted in from a nearby bakery. He sniffed the air in delight and his father smiled.

'It's only about another hour to Archchi's but do you want anything to eat?' Thaththi asked, looking in the rear-view mirror before opening his door.

'A bun and a plantain!' Mythil said quickly. Thaththi disappeared into the bakery and Mythil's mouth watered as he breathed in the wonderful smell of fresh bread. Thaththi was out again soon with two hot, squishy, raisin buns in a paper bag and a fat kolikuttu plantain.

'If you need me just toot the horn,' Thaththi said taking a big bite off a fish bun. Mythil nodded in relief. To be honest, he had been a little worried. The world seemed full of yakas suddenly. He had seen so many since just yesterday. Tooting the horn was a good idea – a sure way of getting attention.

'Do you need anything else?' Thaththi asked before taking another bite. Mythil started to shake his head and then nodded.

'Slippers,' he said. Thaththi smiled. 'Okay, emails first and then slippers,' he said walking away.

Mythil began peeling the ripe yellow plantain. He watched a man walk past the car. Was he a yaka? Would Thaththi have enough time to come out of the shop after he had sounded the horn? Then he realised with relief that the car was iron. They couldn't touch him because he was protected from all sides with iron.

He bit off a small piece of the banana and then sank his teeth into the bun. It was still warm from the oven. He sighed and leaned back savouring each mouthful. After he finished he put the banana skin into the paper bag and folded it into a neat rectangle. He'd lob it at the next rubbish dump they drove past. Ammi was very particular about littering and Mythil knew by now not to throw anything randomly out of car windows.

Mythil pulled out the green yaka ornament from his pocket and had a closer look at it. It didn't look like the usual Sri Lankan yaka masks. For a start it was made from an opaque green glass. The ones he was used to seeing were made of wood and painted in vivid colours. He shook it again. It was definitely broken inside. He put it back in his pocket with a sigh. Now what was he to do with it? Would the yaka woman come after him to get it back? That was a horrifying thought.

He straightened up and watched an old woman walking towards the car through the rear view mirror. She was looking around for something or someone. He looked hard at her eyes. Were they glowing? Was she a yaka? She was too far away to tell. Suddenly Mythil didn't want to know the answer to that. He rolled up his shutter, locked all the doors and looked down at his feet. Blue slippers, he thought. He would ask Thaththi to buy him blue slippers.

From black and white to colour

As they drove into Archchi's place an hour later Mythil forgot about how tight the straps were on his new, bright blue slippers. Ammi and Archchi were at the door to greet him and they both hugged him hard.

Thaththi put his arm around Ammi and she smiled her special smile at him – it wasn't as sunshiny as it usually was but Mythil thought it was pretty good. Archchi's smile for Thaththi was rather small but Mythil didn't care. He felt on top of the world knowing that his parents had made up.

When he wandered out after his bath a little while later wearing his favourite faded t-shirt and shorts he found the house a hive of activity. The pantry was full of mouth-watering smells. Mythil checked the pots and pans by the stove. Fried eggplant and onion in a dish of wambatu moju, a golden chicken curry, fried potatoes and garlic, peppery ambul thiyal fish – mmm. He popped a cube of pineapple into his mouth from the salad dish. Lunch was going to be a feast.

Seeli was washing and drying Archchi's best china plates at the pantry sink, Ammi and Thaththi were sweeping and arranging the hall and Archchi was peeling boiled eggs. 'Who's coming to lunch?' Mythil asked Archchi, picking up an eggshell and nibbling at a piece of egg still stuck to it.

'That aunty and uncle at whose place you spent the night,' Archchi said, deftly shelling an egg.

'Why?' Mythil asked, a feeling of dread creeping up his spine. That morning in the shop this must have been the visit he had overheard Thaththi talking about with Uncle Anthony and Aunty Nilmini. Had they found out that the yaka ornament was missing? No, it couldn't be that, they had decided on the visit just as soon as he had taken the ornament. Why were they visiting in such a hurry? Would the yaka woman come too?

'They're helping your Thaththi to find a job,' Archchi said. 'This will be a nice way to say thank you for their help won't it?' she smiled brightly at

Mythil. 'And don't they have a little girl about your age?'

Mythil groaned and Archchi pretended to look stern. 'It'll be good for you to have someone your age to play with,' she said, but she didn't sound very convincing. Mythil thought that perhaps she wasn't sure about them either.

'They should be here soon,' Archchi went on. 'Go and change your clothes and then come and help me.'

'What's wrong with these clothes?' Mythil asked pulling his t-shirt by its hem. Even as he did that his thumb went through a hole in it. Archchi looked at him sternly, putting her hands on her hips and Mythil scooted off to his room with a grin.

What should he wear? That girl had been wearing posh clothes for the house. But then she was a girl. Girls did that. He chose a pair of faded blue denim shorts that had once belonged to his cousin Chetiya and a red cotton t-shirt that was nice and worn but still looked good. He tried out different hairstyles on his wet hair and then settled for his usual – parted at the right – and sauntered out.

Archchi whistled when she saw him. 'Very nice!' she said winking at Mythil. He grinned at her wishing he could whistle too. 'Now help me shell these hard boiled eggs,' she said.

Archchi always looked like she was expecting company so she never needed to go and change especially for visitors. Today she was wearing an orange lungi and a cream blouse. Orange was her favourite colour. Her long white-grey hair was neatly combed in a long plait and Mythil knew that when the visitors came Archchi would deftly twist the plait into a neat bun at the back of her head.

Mythil practiced his whistle but only got a whooshing sound. 'Now don't forget your manners at the table,' Archchi said suddenly looking at the clock. 'Don't talk with your mouth full and remember to let the visitors serve first.'

At the thought of spending the whole day with Aunty Nilmini and her family Mythil felt gloomy and anxious. By now the yaka woman may have told them that the ornament was missing. Should he confess to the theft now or wait and see what happened?

He finished shelling an egg and then slipped away to check on his parents. They weren't in the hall anymore or in any of the rooms. Mythil stopped in the corridor to look at the ornamental masks that hung there. They were rather dusty and lifeless. None of them looked like the tree yaka or the shop yaka.

He wandered out into the hall again. Looking out of one of the windows he saw his mother cutting some flowers for a vase and handing them to his father to hold. They were deep in conversation but it didn't look like a fight. If he told them what he had done that would upset them all over again. Mythil decided to wait till later.

Back in the kitchen he picked up another egg to peel. Should he tell Archchi about the yaka he saw? She had thought he was mistaken the last time. Perhaps she was right? Perhaps the smoke from the incense burner had distorted his vision? Perhaps he *hadn't* seen a yaka on the pavement that morning. He sighed all over the eggs and got shooed away by Archchi.

First, she sent him to put some rice in the bird and squirrel feeders in the garden. Then she sent him out to tuck the eggshells into the beds of anthuriums (Archchi said that eggshells were good manure for anthuriums). He was out in the side garden finishing this last task when Seeli came running up to him from her kitchen, looking cautiously towards the house.

'Podi Baby,' she whispered with the air of a conspirator. 'I went to the jungle early morning today and I left a fruit puja at the big rock – just to be safe.' She giggled like a school-girl and rushed back to her kitchen which was billowing smoke at that moment. Wondering what to make of it, Mythil followed her.

'How would a fruit puja help?' he asked Seeli, pinching a handful of freshly scraped coconut and popping it in his mouth. She was vigorously stirring something over the fire – something with chillies in it, because Mythil was soon coughing. She motioned for him to leave her kitchen. 'I'll get scolded!' she whispered theatrically and turned back to her cooking. So Mythil returned to the pantry no wiser to the benefits of a fruit puja and still worried about the visit.

Archchi and Mythil had just finished decorating the yellow rice with the boiled eggs and fried raisins and cashews, when there was a toot at the gate. Seeli went running to open the gate, muttering that Jamis was still not back from going to the shops for some last minute things.

The visitors came in a big white Honda. Thaththi and Ammi went out into the driveway to greet them. They had changed into khaki slacks and t-shirts and looked good together, Mythil thought. At first he hung back with Archchi but she soon finished her chores in the pantry.

'Come along Mythie-boy,' she said twisting her hair into a bun and hurrying to join his parents in the garden. So Mythil was forced to follow.

Out in the garden the Honda was pulling up underneath a shady kottamba tree. As the car doors opened Mythil heaved a sigh of relief. Only Uncle Anthony, Aunty Nilmini and the girl from that morning got out of the car. The yaka woman hadn't come with them.

The girl grinned and waved at him in a familiar way. She seemed to be around Mythil's age and was about half an inch taller than him. She had changed her clothes and was now in a pair of blue-green long shorts and a white t-shirt with blue beads and silver sequins sewn on it in the pattern of a butterfly. She had a smart little blue bag slung over her shoulder and a blue butterfly clip in her short hair.

'And this is Ianthi,' Aunty Nilmini told Archchi and Ammi as Uncle Anthony locked the car with an electronic key tag thing that beeped and made the Honda's lights blink.

Show-off, Mythil thought. He leaned against Archchi and looked at his new slippers. Aunty Nilmini had pushed her sunglasses up on her hair and looked like a huge beetle he thought. He wondered again whether anyone could have seen him steal the yaka ornament, which was now safely hidden under an upturned flower pot in one of Archchi's anthurium beds. No one mentioned anything about it but his feeling of gloom only worsened as he followed them inside.

Jamis the gardener had plucked several golden thambilies from the trees in the garden that morning and the visitors enjoyed the sweet king coconut water. They sat in the hall which had large windows looking out on the garden on three sides. Mythil perched on a windowsill behind Archchi even though there were plenty of chairs to sit on. Archchi turned around and tried to signal him with her eyes to sit on a chair but he pretended not to notice. He did *not* want to talk to Ianthi, he thought, looking out of the window. What would he say to her?

The grown-ups conversation was a little stilted at first. Aunty Nilmini did most of the talking. She wore gold hoop earrings that flashed as brightly as her eyes when she spoke. She explained that she was the chairperson of a child welfare organisation and was hoping to meet the people who ran a branch in this area. She asked for directions to the office and Thaththi explained how she could get there.

Then Ammi asked Uncle Anthony how he came to Sri Lanka and he explained that he belonged to a small community of people with Chinese ancestry who had come and settled down in Sri Lanka over a century ago. But he had attended a university in Hong Kong and returned to practice law in Sri Lanka.

'So actually I am more Sri Lankan than Chinese,' he said. 'I love hot curry and sambol. You won't find many people from Hong Kong enjoying that!' Then the conversation turned to food, and talk flowed more smoothly.

Eventually they all sat down to lunch at the table. It was a jolly meal and Mythil gradually forgot that Ammi and Thaththi had had a fight the day before. He even overcame his shyness enough to pass Ianthi the chicken curry and ask her if she needed more water.

After the lunch dishes were cleared away, he helped Archchi serve the pudding by plonking the teaspoons into each dish after she had filled it with a slice of pudding and a generous serving of custard.

'I think I like this pudding Archchi,' Mythil told her after savouring his first mouthful. 'It isn't like wattakka at all – not like when you eat it with rice.'

Everyone laughed and Mythil felt rather elated that he had made the grown-ups laugh.

Then Aunty Nilmini told Mythil casually: 'Why don't you tell us about the adventures you've been having, Mythil?'

Mythil blushed. He mashed the pudding in his bowl with a spoon without saying anything.

'Go on, Mythil,' Ammi coaxed with a smile on her face.

He looked around the table and they all looked back at him expectantly. Did everyone know about him seeing yakas? Had Thaththi told them when he went back upstairs to call Ammi and he was down in the shop? He felt a little angry at that. It felt like his father had betrayed him.

'Adventures about . . . about the yakas?' Mythil ventured trying to stall for time. Or had Ianthi's parents overheard Thaththi's phone conversation with Ammi that morning?

'Oh yes, I love scary stories!' Aunty Nilmini exclaimed. 'Tell us the story from the beginning Mythil. Please?'

Mythil's cheeks were burning. From the corner of his eye he could see that Ianthi was looking at him. She must think him a baby to believe in yakas. He took a quick look around the table. Only Archchi and Uncle Anthony weren't looking at him – she was serving him more pudding. Everyone else looked eager to hear his tale. Even Ianthi. There was no escape, he thought in a panic.

Okay, you can do this, he told himself. If you keep it as brief as possible and don't go into too many descriptions it will be all right. Don't make it sound too fantastic.

Taking a deep breath he plunged into the story, his voice shaking a little at first. He started the story from when he saw the yaka on the tree. But he decided to limit his story to two yakas – the tree yaka and the shop yaka. He didn't mention the fruit seller outside Ianthi's house.

'So the two yakas didn't look alike?' Aunty Nilmini asked when Mythil had finished his story. She looked very serious and there was a little crease between her eyebrows.

'No,' Mythil said pushing the leftover pudding around in his bowl as he pictured the two yakas again. 'The first one was small and dark and wild-looking. The er. . . one in the shop was green.'

Aunty Nilmini looked very grave. She turned to exchange a worried glance with Uncle Anthony but he was scraping the last of the pudding from his bowl and missed the look. Ianthi tried to catch her mother's eye but Aunty Nilmini turned back to Mythil.

'The first yaka was in black and white, no? And the second one was in colour?' she asked. This was a strange way of putting it but Mythil nodded.

He couldn't see the point in her question.

'The first yaka was just black with white teeth and eyes,' he said in a small voice. Perhaps Aunty Nilmini was an expert on yakas? Would that explain why she had one running her shop? He had decided that she herself couldn't be a yaka because he hadn't seen her yaka face.

Looking around at the adults he began to feel a little awkward. This was the first time he had been listened to by every adult in the room and Mythil didn't like the way they all wore such serious, funeral-faces.

Seeing a yaka was scary enough. But was it so bad that it worried grown-ups? Archchi had only laughed at him and told him he hadn't seen a yaka. Thaththi had said he was too old to believe in them. Now everyone looked so serious.

Ammi caught his eye, winked and gave a little smile. She had noticed how worried he looked. 'So that's why you needed new slippers, no?' she said with a grin. 'Your old ones are still in the jungle.' On cue the mood around the table lightened.

'I used to hate getting new slippers,' Aunty Nilmini said pouring herself some more water. 'I think everyone does. I even knew a girl who used to get her elder sister to wear her new slippers for a week until they were worn out a bit. Of course she had to make her sister's bed for that week to return the favour. And, no – I'm not the elder sister!' Everyone laughed again.

Mythil felt a little relieved after that. Things never looked too bad when the grown-ups were laughing. Archchi offered everyone second helpings of pudding.

'Oh yes, thank you, I think I'll have some more,' Uncle Anthony said passing his dessert bowl to her for a refill. Ianthi whispered something to him and he laughed.

'No secrets in company Ianthi,' he told her, playfully tweaking her nose. 'Ianthi says it's my third serving of pudding.' He smiled ruefully. 'She's right but it's so delicious that I think I'll have some more anyway.' Archchi beamed at him. Mythil couldn't help smiling at Uncle Anthony too. He had said just the right thing to make Archchi happy.

'Will you have some more too Nils?' Uncle Anthony asked his wife. But Aunty Nilmini said she was stuffed and would walk in the garden for a bit. Ianthi didn't want any pudding either but she remained at the table with her father.

'Mythil, would you mind keeping Aunty Nilmini company while I help Archchi to clear the table?' Ammi asked him collecting the empty dishes.

'I'll help you Aunty,' Ianthi said picking up the big custard jug carefully and heading for the pantry. Mythil got up from the table reluctantly making a face at his mother which only she could see.

'Go on! Now don't make a fuss,' she told him with her eyes and he went out, dragging his feet. 'She likes flowers!' Ammi called out after him, 'You could show her Archchi's anthuriums.'

Mythil found Aunty Nilmini admiring a patch of blue flowers under a bower of yellow ones.

'Isn't this beautiful?' she asked him bending towards the flowers and touching them lightly with her fingers. 'I love bright colours like this in the garden! But I do hate anthuriums. They seem so artificial and plastic-like, don't you think?'

Mythil hesitated. Archchi loved them. 'The anthuriums are Archchi's favourites,' he said stoically, picking off a dried leaf from the bower and flicking it into a flowerbed.

'Oh look at that stream!' Aunty Nilmini exclaimed pulling her sunglasses down over her eyes and striding towards it. Perhaps she hadn't heard his comment? He followed her, kicking at imaginary stones on the lawn with his new slippers. 'Streams are such happy, bubbly things no? You can't be sad listening to a stream,' she said. Mythil looked across at the jungle remembering his first yaka encounter.

'Is it very far from here?' Aunty Nilmini asked him and he realised with a little start that she must have been staring at him again. He couldn't read her eyes because they were hidden behind the sunglasses. He could only see himself in the reflection. 'I mean the place you saw the yaka?' she asked.

Mythil shook his head his mouth suddenly dry. He didn't know why but he was feeling strange again. He could feel the hairs on the back of his neck rising. Was he sensing danger? Was that tree-yaka hiding somewhere close by? He couldn't see anything odd in the trees across the stream.

Aunty Nilmini was silent for a while. She too looked out at the trees in front of them, shading her face from the hot afternoon sun. 'Will you be too scared to go there again?' she asked a tiny smile turning up the corners of her mouth. 'With me?' she bent down and picked up a pebble.

I don't have iron on me, Mythil thought. But he didn't want to tell her that. 'Shall I ask my father to come too?' he asked instead trying to smile back but knowing that it was rather a weak effort.

'Oh, no, no! He's having a nice comfortable chat after lunch now,' Aunty Nilmini said, dropping her hand to her side with a slap and sounding disappointed. Her shoulders drooped and she threw the pebble sharply into the water. 'Never mind. I just thought you wouldn't mind showing me the yaka tree, that's all,' she said turning back towards the house.

Mythil squirmed a bit. 'We could go and have a quick look,' he said falteringly. After all, he wouldn't be alone. Usually in yaka stories, the human was alone. And if she was a yaka expert he would be all right with her, wouldn't he?

'Are you sure?' Aunty Nilmini whipped back around to him with a bright smile. She didn't give him time to reply. Hugging herself she did a little jig in one spot and said, 'Ooh, how exciting!'

Mythil smiled mirthlessly and dug his hands deep into his pockets. 'Yes,' he said, looking back at the house, 'it is.' It was a bit too exciting, he thought, but he didn't say that out loud.

Afternoon walk

Mythil licked his dry lips and wiped a bead of sweat from his forehead with his thumb. He would have felt better if he could tell someone where they were going – just in case. He saw Seeli staring at them from the kitchen doorway and felt better. She would see them heading into the jungle. If they didn't return she'd know where they went. And she had left a fruit puja too she said – perhaps that was a good thing. He wished he had asked her more about it now.

Taking off his new slippers Mythil waded into the stream, his whole being focused on the jungle. Aunty Nilmini slipped off her leather sandals and picked them up in one hand. With the other she held her long yellow skirt around her knees to avoid getting it wet.

'Oooh, these rocks under the water are quite slippery,' Aunty Nilmini said her arms whirling about like a windmill as she tried to keep her balance.

Mythil hardly noticed. He was looking up at the branches that were gently swaying in the breeze. It was that time of the day again, when yakas rested on trees, he thought. The jungle was quiet.

He could hear Aunty Nilmini splashing along behind him. As they got to the opposite bank Mythil dropped his slippers on to the ground and groped for them with wet feet. He slipped them on without taking his eyes off the trees ahead.

'Do you remember the way?' Aunty Nilmini called out from behind him, bending down to put on her own sandals.

'Shhhhhhhh!' he wanted to say, but didn't. Instead Mythil nodded and pressed on into the jungle, hoping his new slippers wouldn't start squeaking. They did of course and he had to limp to minimise the noise.

'Ah, it's so much cooler among the trees!' Aunty Nilmini said. Mythil didn't reply.

He realised that there was actually a faint trail as they walked along. When he had dashed into the jungle that first time – was it only yesterday? – he must have run along it without being aware. This was probably the route Seeli took when she went to leave her pujas for the bahirawaya. Did Jamis the gardener come this way to gather firewood, he wondered.

They soon came to the huge banyan tree and there, a few yards away from it, were his old slippers. He looked at them carefully. Had they been moved? Aunty Nilmini picked them up before he could decide.

'Are these the slippers you left behind?' she asked with a laugh. It wasn't a kind laugh, he thought. Her sunglasses were pushed up into her hair again and he could see her eyes.

He nodded, reaching out for them. The clearing seemed the same as when he had left it – except that there was no yaka of course, he thought, looking at the bahirawaya carving and a woven watti of fruit at the foot of the great rock. Seeli's fruit puja.

'Can you see the yaka now?' Aunty Nilmini whispered loudly, bending towards him with her hand cupped around her mouth and a smile playing on her lips.

Mythil was hurt. Was she laughing at him? With her sunglasses up on her head again she looked more like a giant bug than ever, he thought. Like a bug played by a bad actor in a school play. Mythil noticed that a corner of her skirt had got wet and felt a smidgen of satisfaction.

She turned to look at the banyan tree. 'Is this your yaka tree?' Mythil was about to correct her when his eyes darted up to the tree on which the yaka had been perched the day before. *Oh help!* There it was again, peering down at them and making awful faces at Aunty Nilmini.

Mythil took in a sharp breath and dropped his slippers. 'What is it?' Aunty Nilmini asked. Mythil's first impulse was to run but what about Aunty Nilmini? He couldn't just leave her. She was looking directly up at the dark, grimacing yaka now but didn't seem to be able to see it.

'I don't see a yaka – do you?' she asked Mythil throwing up her hands and pursing her lips in disappointment. 'Now, don't you think you may have been mistaken about seeing one?'

Mythil didn't reply. His mind was still reeling from the fact that the yaka was there on the tree in front of him. It was definitely a yaka. Not a village boy playing a prank. Then he relaxed a little. He was with a grown up after all. He should be safe shouldn't he?

Aunty Nilmini shook her head at him with the disappointed look still on her face. 'There's no shame in admitting that you made a mistake Mythil,' she said. The speckles of sunlight that filtered through the branches overhead made her gold earrings sparkle.

She walked away from him looking up at the other trees and peering into the thicket with her back to him.

Mythil didn't take his eyes off the yaka. It was making some very grotesque faces at the retreating Aunty Nilmini and suddenly, Mythil found it hard to keep a straight face.

'Hello! Are there any yakas out here?' Aunty Nilmini called out and the yaka did a somersault on its branch. Mythil giggled. Aunty Nilmini turned towards him and to hide his smile from her Mythil bent down to pick up his slippers again.

'I don't see any yakas – do you?' she asked again. Mythil smothered another giggle and pretended to cough.

'We all have our own demons to battle with, Mythil,' Aunty Nilmini said as she walked towards the banyan tree. She bent down and picked up a charred clay pot from the pile at the foot of the banyan tree. 'Even adults like us,' she said over her shoulder. 'There are so many things to be afraid of in life. But the trick is to face those fears. Running away won't solve them.'

She was starting to sound a lot like his Math teacher in school when he got a sum wrong. This made it very easy to stop listening to her.

Careful to keep his face turned away from Aunty Nilmini, Mythil watched the yaka instead, secretly smiling at its antics. The creature turned around and waggled its behind at Aunty Nilmini and Mythil had to bite his lips to stop from giggling out loud. But after a while the creature seemed to get tired of making funny faces.

Its teeth gleamed white against a dark, bear-like face. It seemed to have too many incisor-teeth in its mouth, Mythil thought. It suddenly scowled and stood up. The smile on Mythil's face froze. Was it going to jump down?

Aunty Nilmini placed a hand on his shoulder and made him jump. 'Don't you think I'm right?' she asked him a little puzzled at his reaction. She gazed up at the spot he had been looking at but seemed not to see anything.

'We have to go now,' Mythil said as evenly as he could. With his old slippers in one hand he reached out with the other, grabbed Aunty Nilmini's wrist and dragged her away, back towards the stream.

'Mythil, wait!' she said impatiently, her wet feet slipping a little in her sandals, but he didn't care. He pulled her along and she followed with a half impatient, half amused look on her face.

Just as they reached the stream she managed to loosen his grip on her hand. 'Mythil, what's wrong?' she asked, turning him around to face her. 'Did you see the yaka after all?'

Mythil avoided her searching eyes. He looked across the stream at the house. 'It's just time to go back home now,' he said sullenly pulling away from her. 'That's all. They'll be worried.'

He ignored Aunty Nilmini's reproachful tone as she asked him if he had heard anything they had just been discussing.

Pffffff! he thought, what *they* had been discussing? She had just been going on by herself, hadn't she? What did *she* know about yakas? She didn't even believe in them, couldn't even see them and yet here she was making fun of him!

He waded through the stream, slippers and all and didn't even stop when Aunty Nilmini said, 'Oh dear, I forgot to take my sandals off!' Serves her right, he thought as he headed for the house.

Battle of wills

Mythil left Aunty Nilmini to find her own way to the hall, feeling angry at her. He was sure she had been laughing at him. How silly he had been to tell the grown-ups about the yakas, he thought angrily as he headed for the pantry.

He found Archchi packing some of her famous homemade mango chutney in a bottle for the guests to take home. 'Don't pack it all for them, Archchi!' he said crossly, 'I like it too. You're always giving away things that I like, to the cats, to the squirrels, for strangers who come from nowhere.' Archchi smiled but wisely said nothing.

'Urrgh! They make me mad!' Mythil growled, not staying to explain whether by 'they' he meant the visitors or the cats or the squirrels. He kicked off his new slippers, jumped into his old ones and stormed outside leaving Archchi smiling to herself in the pantry.

The adults' voices wafted out into the garden from the hall. Mythil pricked his ears. Were they talking about him? He crept under the hall window and sat on the cement lip of the dry, two-foot rainwater drain that ran around the house.

Aunty Nilmini was speaking. 'It's easy to see that he's worried about your quarrels. So because he can't speak to you about what's really worrying him ...'

Ammi's voice interrupted a little defensively. 'Why do you say that? We're always there for him to talk to. He knows he can speak to us about anything.'

'I'm not saying that you aren't there for him,' Aunty Nilmini said. 'But there's obviously some reason why he thinks he's seeing yakas.'

'And it's getting worse, isn't it Mummy?' Ianthi piped up. 'Now he's seeing them in colour so that means they're getting more real ...'

'Ianthi!' That was Uncle Anthony's quiet voice. 'Don't interrupt when

Mummy's talking.'

Outside the window Mythil curled his lip in contempt. So he couldn't even count on Ianthi to believe his yaka stories just because she was a kid like him, he thought. She was on the side of the adults. None of them believed him.

'We can't generalise like that Ianthi,' Aunty Nilmini said a little reproachfully. 'Ianthi's hoping to be a psychologist when she grows up,' she explained. 'So I talk to her about the subjects I'm studying . . .'

'You mean you're *not* a psychologist?' Ammi asked a hint of sarcasm in her tone. And outside Mythil silently cheered that Aunty Nilmini was being put in her place.

'I'm doing a long distance course,' Aunty Nilmini said evenly. Mythil thought she sounded a little offended. 'I'll need to think about Mythil's case. Each case has to be looked at individually before any judgements can be made. . .'

Thaththi cut in then, 'Nilmini, we asked you to help because of your background in counselling. How serious do you think this problem is? Do you think it's a passing phase and we should just ignore it or do you think it's serious?'

Mythil kicked out in frustration and stubbed his toe on the opposite wall of the storm water drain. He dropped into the drain, stifling a yelp of pain. He was not mental! Why couldn't Thaththi believe him he thought angrily blinking tears from his eyes.

Aunty Nilmini spoke again. Holding his toe Mythil crouched on the lip of the drain straining upwards to hear her better. 'Children are the ones who are affected the most when parents have arguments,' she was saying. 'Of course all parents do argue and that's natural but if their arguments get to a level that makes the child feel insecure . . .'

'Like when Mythil was dragged off to your place last night?' Ammi choked out.

'Well, don't pretend you had nothing to do with that,' Thaththi's voice said getting louder. 'I told you . . .'

Mythil felt horrified and ashamed. Now they were fighting because of him he thought, groaning and rubbing his sweaty forehead on his palms.

They were fighting because he was seeing those wretched spirits. And they were fighting in front of strangers!

For a minute he wished he didn't have parents. It would have been so much better to have been an orphan, he thought. But it was only a fleeting thought. He knew deep down that he loved his parents. Even though they made him so angry.

Then Uncle Anthony interrupted, 'For Mythil's sake let's see what can be done.' Mythil buried his face in his hands. His parents were acting like spoilt children. And Ianthi's parents were advising them! Could he ever forget the shame of it?

Aunty Nilmini went on, a slight note of triumph in her voice. She was happy that they were fighting, Mythil thought angrily. 'When parents get wrapped up in their arguments to a degree that the child feels neglected or alone he will often either act up or tell stories just to get the parents' attention back on him ...'

Mythil was furious. Now she's making Ammi and Thaththi believe I'm making it up, he thought. That's it, he thought bitterly. I'm never going to tell them anything ever again. What's the point? They don't believe me. And it only makes their fighting worse.

A breeze ruffled his hair and the curtain fluttered out of the open window. Mythil wondered whether he could peer in through the window using the curtain for cover. But just as he was about to crouch under the window a figure appeared around the corner and stopped at the sight of him.

'Hi!' It was Ianthi wearing a big grin on her face. Was she laughing at him too? He made a rude face at her and jumped over the drain.

Walking away from her towards the other side of the house, he willed her not to follow. Would she think he had been spying on the grown-ups? Mythil groaned in embarrassment. Now she would think he was just as childish as his parents. Why was everything going wrong? There was an old araliya tree in the middle of the lawn. He pulled himself mid-way up the tree and straddled a branch.

He looked down. Ianthi had followed him. At first she ignored Mythil. She stood under the tree adjusting her blue butterfly clip and looking around at the fresh araliya flowers that had fallen on the lawn after Jamis the gardener had swept it that morning. She picked up a flower and twirled it between her fingers, making it spiral down on to the grass. Then she squinted up at him.

'So what are you going to do about the yaka?' she asked him.

Ianthi shaded her eyes from the sun and a blue butterfly bracelet glinted on her wrist. She must have left her handbag in the house, Mythil thought distractedly. He was trying to figure out whether she was on the adults' side or not.

'Aren't you going to tell me?' she asked a smile playing on her lips. 'I won't tell anyone.'

Mythil was on his guard at once. He glared at her. 'Oh, come on! I heard what you were saying in there. You don't believe I saw a yaka any more than they do,' he accused her. He ignored her when she looked reproachfully at him and they were silent for a while.

'Why don't you go back inside,' he said jeeringly. 'Be with your mother. She doesn't believe me either.'

Ianthi pursed her lips into a pout. 'I can be where I want to,' the girl said with spirit. She seemed to be considering what to do for a moment and then, in a matter of seconds had pulled herself up the tree to a branch on level with him.

'This is my tree . . .' Mythil began, but Ianthi interrupted him.

'It's your grandmother's tree,' she said lifting her chin defiantly.

'So? That's as good as my tree,' Mythil defended. How dare she come and mess up his life with her airs and graces?

'Well if it is your tree and your house, then you are the host and you have to be polite to me because I am the guest.' She said it firmly and with authority and Mythil was taken aback. He was silent for a while. What she said was true. It was just that morning that Archchi had told him to mind his manners and Ammi was always going on and on about how he should be more hospitable to the children who came home for her tuition classes. But he was angry.

'Why don't you go back there and tell them I'm being rude to you then. You're just like them,' he indicated the adults in the hall. 'You belong with them. You don't believe I saw a yaka either.'

'I *do* believe,' she said her chin sticking out stubbornly again. 'I'm not in there with them now am I? I can't help what they're talking about. I came out to try and find you and . . . and to tell you that if you're going to do anything about the yaka, I'd like to help,' she said.

This unsettled Mythil. Perhaps Ianthi was different from her parents. Come to think of it she didn't look much like them. She had her father's eyes but she wasn't as fair as him or as dark as her mother. And her hair was black, straight and stopped just short of her shoulders. But Aunty Nilmini had long curly hair and Uncle Anthony's was short and grey.

He decided to switch the conversation to a safer topic. 'Was that a neek-neek . . . sorry er. . . I mean a PlayStation I saw at your place?'

'It's a DS Lite,' Ianthi said and Mythil fell silent. Was that a model number? Was it better than a PlayStation? He didn't want to ask.

There was a bunch of araliya flowers within reach. Ianthi reached out, picked a flower and sent it twirling down towards the lawn below them. She had on a pair of blue sandals and Mythil noticed that the big toe on her right foot was bandaged. They watched the flower land on the grass a few feet away.

'I accidentally dropped it and it stopped working,' she went on. 'But the warranty's still valid so my dad said he'd get a replacement for me the next time we go to Hong Kong. Do you have any games we can play?'

Mythil knew she meant electronic games. 'Not here,' he mumbled. Perhaps she would think he had one at home. He didn't want to say that his parents couldn't afford one. And that he only had two old neek-neek games that his cousins had outgrown. And a few computer games on his father's old computer which he could only use when Thaththi wasn't working on it.

Ianthi didn't say anything and Mythil's cheeks burned. She probably guesses I don't have one, he thought.

He was wracking his brains for a way of changing the subject again when there was an interruption. It was Jamis the gardener.

'What are you doing breaking flowers and messing up the lawn like this? I just swept it,' he said in his hoarse rasping voice. Using the ekel broom he jabbed at the flowers on the lawn. They stuck neatly to the ekels.

'Get down from that tree the both of you,' he scolded. 'You'll get into trouble for breaking flowers.'

'It's not your tree. . .' Ianthi ventured, quite bravely, Mythil thought. He wasn't exactly afraid of Jamis and his sudden flare-ups but he and his cousins usually kept out of the gardener's way.

'Get down from that tree, I tell you,' Jamis said flinging the broom down on to the ground in a fury. 'I'll go and tell them now and you'll get scolded.'

'Go and tell them Jamis,' Mythil retorted, his heart racing a little. Not wanting to show Ianthi that he was scared, Mythil managed to keep his voice steady. 'But you'll be the one to get in trouble. This is my father's friend's daughter. They're our guests and you'll get into trouble for scolding her.'

Jamis considered this sullenly his wrinkled old face glaring up at them. 'You're putting the little miss in danger, Podi Baby,' he said at last in a wheedling voice. 'She could fall and break an arm.'

But he didn't care about Ianthi breaking an arm and she and Mythil both knew it. That was just a feeble effort on his part to scare them into climbing down.

'That's my look out,' Mythil said scornfully. 'Go away Jamis. Leave us alone.'

'Yes, we'll take our chances, thank you very much.' Ianthi added impudently.

Glowering at her, Jamis picked up the broom and retreated, muttering under his breath as he went. 'If they fall it's not my fault . . .' they heard him saying.

Mythil felt like crowing! He'd won that argument. Not even his quick witted cousin Chetiya had ever done that. He and Ianthi exchanged gleeful grins.

'Who was that?' Ianthi asked.

'Just Jamis the gardener,' Mythil replied. 'He's always in a bad mood.'

'He sounded quite mad!'

Mythil laughed. 'Yes, he does sound mad sometimes. People in the village are scared to come into our garden because they think he's mad. He's better than any watchdog though.'

Ianthi sent another flower twirling down and stuck her tongue out at Jamis' retreating back.

'So what are you going to do about the yaka?' she asked again.

Mythil considered this. He was feeling quite brave after his victory over Jamis. 'I'll have to face him,' he said. 'I'll have to find some iron first and then I'll go back into the jungle and fight him.'

'Why iron and where will you find it from?' Ianthi asked.

'Why iron?' Mythil asked scornfully. 'Because that's how you protect yourself from a yaka!' He had forgotten that he had only learnt this yesterday from Seeli. 'I bet there's lots of iron in the shed,' Mythil said.

Now seemed as good a time as any to go and check it out. He leapt on to the grass and ran towards the kitchen area. He heard Ianthi jump down too and this time rather than being annoyed that she was following him, he felt rather gratified.

He peered around a corner of the house like people did on TV when they were in an adventure. He saw old Jamis disappearing around the corner with a folded up newspaper and knew he was going to sit in the ancient guardhouse by the gate and snooze with the papers. He squinted at the kitchen yard. No one seemed to be around.

'Come on,' he said and sprinted towards the shed door with Ianthi following close behind.

On the trail

Mythil put his hand on the latch of the shed door. It had rotted away at the bottom and been patched with a sheet of aluminium but there was a hole in the corner big enough for rats to get in. Mythil's mouth went dry. He hated everything about rats; their prickly fur and those horrible hairless tails.

'Are you scared of rats?' he whispered to Ianthi.

'No,' she said. But she didn't sound very sure of herself and she looked worried. She *is* scared of them, Mythil thought. But she isn't admitting it. He sighed. That meant he'd have to be the brave one. Mythil squared his shoulders.

'If you are scared of them, you'd better stand back a bit,' he said confidently; far more confidently than he felt. Ianthi wet her dry lips with a pink tongue but stayed where she was.

A small voice in his head told Mythil that he was being a silly show-off but he ignored the voice, opened the door a crack and stepped in. Nothing moved, much to his relief. But it was so dark inside after the bright afternoon light that it took him a while to see anything.

'It's okay.' He motioned for her to follow and shut the door behind her so that no one would guess they were there.

The shed smelt strongly of dust, smoke and rotting leather. Smoke from the kitchen fire had made the walls inside sooty near the window. For a minute Mythil wondered whether he was doing the right thing by bringing a visitor to the shed. It wasn't the sort of place you took people to if you wanted to impress them. But that was just a fleeting thought. Soon he was looking around the shed.

The single window was small, barred, mesh-enclosed and covered in cobwebs so most of the room was in sinister-looking shadows. In one corner was a stack of beams and planks of all sizes and shapes. There were cobwebby racks along the walls and in the middle of the room was an old enamel bathtub filled with boxes and odds and ends. Seeya's fishing rods and reels, two ancient cart wheels, rusted spades and wheelbarrows and old leather suitcases filled the racks.

'Now look for anything iron that's easy to carry,' Mythil said moving towards the back of the shed. He almost tripped over a bunch of king coconuts.

Something small scuttled away and he had a strong suspicion that it was a cockroach. Ianthi stepped back. She'd heard the scuffling noise too. But then she seemed to pull herself together. Raising her chin defiantly, she bravely stepped away from the door and moved towards the tub.

Mythil groped his way to the rack at the back and opened an old biscuit tin. Inside it were rusty fishhooks and lures. He tried to pick up a hook but pricked his finger. He drew his hand back sucking at the wound. If Ianthi hadn't been there he would probably have said Ouch! at the very least.

Something bigger than a cockroach scuttled away towards a corner and Mythil stepped back hurriedly. It could have been a rat or a snake. It's just a rat, it's just a rat, he told himself. He hated snakes worse than rats.

He spotted a small penknife in a corner of the box he was still carrying and carefully picked it up. When he put the box down and unfolded the knife he saw that the silver blade was dull but strong. The wooden handle was quite worn, but had a beautifully carved dragon on it. This will do nicely, he thought, folding it and slipping it into his pocket. It looked impressive and he hoped he'd be able to scare the yaka with it.

It was Ianthi who found the box of nails. She stubbed her toe on something and gave a small yelp. It was her wounded toe.

'Are you okay?' Mythil asked, walking back to her. Ianthi nodded again though Mythil could tell by the way her lips were pursed up that the knock must have hurt. She'd hit her toe against an old wooden box. Inside they found rusty old nails sorted in glass bottles according to size. Perfect.

Mythil began filling his pockets with the biggest nails he could find. To his surprise Ianthi started to do the same. 'What are you doing?' Mythil asked her.

'I'm coming with you,' she said simply. He didn't argue. She was different from other girls, he thought. She didn't mind musty sheds and she didn't cry when she was hurt.

'What exactly does a yaka do?' Ianthi asked. 'Can it kill you?'

'Worse,' Mythil said making a face. 'It can get into your mind and drive you mad.' After Seeli had told him that yakas possess people he remembered seeing a TV programme about a yakadura – a man who drove yakas away. The possessed people always looked mad and sometimes they frothed at the mouth before having the yaka driven away from them.

'Oh,' Ianthi said in a small voice.

'Don't you know anything about yakas?' Mythil asked a little surprised.

'Not much,' Ianthi admitted. 'I always thought they were just stories for kids,' she bit her lip and continued hurriedly. 'I never knew they were real!'

But Mythil hadn't been paying attention. He was examining the penknife again. 'If the knife doesn't scare him, we could throw nails at him,' he said, planning his attack. He folded the blade in and slipped the knife into his pocket. Taking a last look at the glass jars he picked out a huge nail, about three inches long. 'Wow! Look at this beauty!'

They slipped out of the shed and Mythil carefully latched the door. 'Now, into the jungle again. Are you sure you want to come with me?' he asked Ianthi.

She nodded dusting off her white t-shirt. Mythil looked at it worriedly. He knew he'd get into trouble for getting Ianthi all dirty. To his relief her t-shirt didn't look too bad. He dusted his own t-shirt and hands.

Then he had another thought. It was the fishing equipment that gave him the idea. 'We need bait to attract the yaka,' he said. 'You stay here and cough if you see anyone, okay? I'm going to raid the pantry.'

'I'll whistle,' Ianthi said with a grin. Mythil wished for the hundredth time that he could whistle too.

He shot off towards the pantry. Seeli would be dozing in the kitchen now he hoped. And Archchi would have finished making food parcels and joined the visitors in the hall. He peered into the pantry. He had guessed right. It was empty. The food parcels sat neatly wrapped in newspaper on the table. The left-overs had been put away.

What could he use as bait for a yaka? Fresh meat? He opened the freezer. All Archchi had there was frozen fish. That wouldn't do. He closed the door and looked around the pantry. Fruit – like Seeli's fruit puja? But why would a yaka in the jungle need fruit? What about kevili? Yes, Seeli had said that yakas were attracted to the smell of kevili.

Quickly pulling out a paper bag from Archchi's stash in the drawer he put together an assortment of sweetmeats, tied them up and stuffed the bundle into his already bulging pockets.

He ran back to where Ianthi was waiting leaning against a shed wall in the shade. 'Ready?' he asked. She nodded. Even in the shade the afternoon sun was hot. Little bubbles of sweat stood out on her nose.

'One, two, three!' They sprinted across the grass and into the jungle, clearing the stream in a single bound.

Mythil led the way looking over his shoulder to check on Ianthi. She overtook him at one point even though he was running his fastest. But he knew the way and when she made a wrong turn he took the lead calling out to her.

Soon they were at the clearing. They stopped to catch their breath. Clutching a stitch in his side, Mythil pointed at the carving on the rock. 'That's the Bahi . . .' Mythil clapped his hand over his mouth. Seeli had said not to mention their names out loud.

'What? This carving?' Ianthi asked peering at the rock figure. 'That's called a Bahi?' She looked up into the trees. 'Where was the yaka?' she asked Mythil. She didn't seem that interested in the carving.

'I'll show you but you shouldn't mention their real names,' Mythil said 'Although I guess since we want to meet this yaka, it's ok.' He pointed at the branch on which the tree-spirit had been when he came with Aunty Nilmini. The jungle was quiet. 'He's not around now, is he?' she asked. Mythil shook his head.

'Is it always this quiet?' she wanted to know. Mythil was thinking the same thing. There wasn't a single birdsong to be heard. Not a leaf rustled. Ianthi walked over to the banyan tree pushing aside one of the rope-like roots that dangled from its branches. A green parakeet which had been invisible against the leaves of the tree flew away, its wings making a rap-a-tap-a-tap noise in the silence.

'Someone comes here quite often. Look at all these old lamps and the fruit. The fruit's quite fresh,' Ianthi said swatting away the tiny fruit flies that were hovering above the puja.

'That's just Seeli,' Mythil said. 'Archchi's cook.'

'You mean we're not in the middle of the jungle? People come here all the time?' Ianthi asked sounding a little disappointed.

'Not *all* the time,' Mythil said, a little defensively. 'I've never seen anyone here but the yaka. I know the fruits are Seeli's because she told me. But that means other people in the village must know this place too.'

'Perhaps they don't,' Ianthi said. She reached for a dangly root of the banyan tree and tried to swing on it. 'Perhaps Seeli is a yaka and you don't know it.'

'She's not,' Mythil said dismissively. 'I would have seen her eyes glowing if she was a yaka.'

'Maybe she's powerful enough to hide her yaka face from you. Perhaps she was here when you came and she cast a spell on you,' Ianthi said, a mischievous grin lighting up her face as she jumped down from her makeshift swing.

Mythil shook his head impatiently. 'I left her in the garden when I came here and when I returned she was on the kitchen steps. It couldn't have been her. Besides, she was the one who warned me to take iron when I go into the jungle.'

Ianthi had turned back to the faded flowers and charred lamps again. 'So many lamps,' she said softly, almost to herself. 'This is a place people come to with all their troubles.' She looked up at Mythil. 'Is that why you came too? Because you were upset about your parents? Maybe you wanted to see a yaka and so you did ... ?'

'You're asking whether I made it up?' Mythil asked in an icy cold voice.

Ianthi only hesitated for a split second before smiling at him. 'No! No! What I meant was that if you came here wanting to see a yaka and there was one around he might have decided to let you see him. Are yaka's usually invisible?'

Mythil relaxed a little. So she wasn't accusing him of imagining the yakas. 'Yeah, I think they can choose who can see them,' he said, thinking of how he was able to see the yaka and Aunty Nilmini wasn't. 'But I didn't come here looking for a yaka. I was actually more worried about pythons and poachers.'

'Well, if it's not Seeli, and other people come here, there must be traces of them. Like a dropped button or a toffee wrapper or, or something,' Ianthi said tossing the lamp into the pile and wiping her fingers on a tree root.

Mythil approved of this idea. That's what happened in books too. People found clues and that lead them to the suspects. Only in this case his suspect wasn't human so would he leave clues?

They hunted around the clearing floor for anything unusual. Mythil walked over to the other side of the rock and noticed something he'd missed before. There seemed to be another path, very faint, leading out of the clearing and deeper into the jungle. He called Ianthi and pointed it out.

'Shall we follow it?' he asked.

'Yes!' she said her eyes shining at the prospect of this new adventure. Silently they picked their way between the trees. Soon they seemed to be quite deep inside the jungle. At times the underbrush was so thick that it was difficult to see any path. And they were always aware of the eerie silence.

'Where do you think this path will lead to?' Ianthi whispered after a while trying to break the silence. Mythil shrugged and pressed on. The jungle around them seemed to be getting thicker and darker. The branches met overhead so it looked like they were walking in a gloomy tunnel. He pulled out the penknife. Why was it so quiet? Were the animals hiding in fear because there was a yaka around?

'Did you say there are snakes?' Ianthi asked suddenly from behind.

Mythil nodded holding a branch aside for her to get through. 'And poachers, so we should be quiet,' he whispered.

He wasn't really sure there were poachers but it made it all the more exciting to think there were. After a while they came to a stop. The path seemed to go two ways. Both ways looked equally desolate and unused. Branches and creepers swung low across them and made it difficult to make out the paths. In fact, the jungle seemed to swallow these wild trails up a few yards on.

Which way should we go? Mythil wondered. Were these proper paths? Or just animal trails? As they stood at the fork still undecided a strong breeze suddenly blew through the trees and the branches overhead came alive, writhing against the white glare of the sky above.

Mythil had that bad feeling again, as if something terrible was going to happen. He unfolded the penknife and held it in his right hand. Ianthi slipped her hand into his left.

Mythil had just decided to take the trail on the right when Ianthi spoke. 'Perhaps we should turn back,' she said looking over her shoulder at the path they had come on. She tugged at his hand urgently. 'We didn't mark the way we came. Do you know how to get back?'

Mythil turned. The path they had come on didn't look as clear as it had seemed on their way there – every branch was swaying and bending for the wind. His heart began to hammer in his chest. Were they lost? Where was the path that lead back to the bahirawaya's clearing?

And then that strange feeling got stronger again. He gripped Ianthi's hand tightly. Something was going to happen now. He was sure of it. But what *was* it? And then he noticed a branch that wasn't swaying normally like the others. Before he could say anything to Ianthi the yaka leapt out at them, fangs bared.

Mythil screamed and heard Ianthi do the same. She let go of his hand and he could hear her crashing away from him through the undergrowth as the yaka pounced on to him.

Shocking information

Mythil was thrown on his back and he and the yaka somersaulted into the undergrowth. The earth and trees and sky tumbled around and around him and all the time the yaka's hairy face was just inches away from his own. Then they crashed into a tree and fell apart.

Mythil had to stop screaming because he had had the breath knocked out of him. And that was when he realised that the yaka was screaming too. Mythil staggered to his feet dragging himself away from the hairy yaka but it made no move to get up. Instead the creature was writhing on the ground with blue flashes dancing over its body. It looked like it was being electrocuted, Mythil thought in horror.

What was wrong with it, he wondered sitting rooted to the spot. And then Mythil saw it. The hilt of his penknife was buried deep in the creature's forearm. *Oh no!* Mythil thought breaking out into a sweat. The iron in the knife is killing the yaka. He hadn't realised until then how deadly a knife could be. If the creature died, it would be all Mythil's fault, he thought in a panic.

He reached forward to pull the knife out but just then the creature moved. With a trembling hand the yaka yanked the blade out by its wooden handle and flung it away with a terrible groan. The blue lights stopped and Mythil heaved a sigh of relief. The yaka groaned again and sat up, swaying a little as if it was disoriented.

Mythil scrambled back halfway into a thick bush not sure what to expect now. The yaka bared its teeth at Mythil but it was a feeble effort to keep the human boy away. Clutching its wounded arm the creature stumbled to its feet and staggered away into the jungle moaning piteously. Soon the trees had swallowed him up and Mythil was left alone in the middle of thick undergrowth.

He could still hear the creature's groans from where he sat. Was it badly hurt? Would it come back for him? Would its moans attract other yakas? This last thought terrified him. Mythil leapt to the spot where the knife had been thrown. It was his only weapon against the yakas and he didn't want to lose it.

Oh help! And he needed to find Ianthi too, he thought, forcing his way into another thick bush. Where had she got to by now? Would she have the sense to stay in one place and wait to be found or would she wander around in circles?

He scrabbled around for the knife despairing of ever finding it again. His fingers brushed against dry earth, twigs and stones and finally closed around the knife handle. Safe at last, he thought as he snatched it up.

Now what? Should he go in search of Ianthi? Yes, that was the first thing to do. He made his way to the fork in the paths and then stopped. He had no idea where she was. Which path had she taken? What if she had strayed from the trail? He might get lost too, trying to find her.

Mythil looked down the path that he and Ianthi had taken to get to this point. Now that the trees were still he could see that it was much clearer than both the path taken by the yaka and the one Ianthi may have taken. He felt sure he could find his own way back home from where he stood. Should he go home and tell his parents?

It took him seconds to decide. No way! He'd be in a lot of trouble – no doubt about that. What about going after the yaka? It was hurt. This may be my only chance to overpower it, he told himself, gripping the knife with sweaty hands. My only chance to find out how to make myself stop seeing yakas.

He looked at the trees and creepers that closed in tightly around him. A faint path was visible between the shrubs here and there. That must have been the way the yaka went. He could hear its groans getting further and further away so he hurried after it, jumping over moss-covered rocks and gnarled roots, and ducking behind trees whenever the groans got louder.

He soon caught up with it; a dark shape lumbering deeper into the jungle. It looked so much like a small bear, he thought. The thing seemed to have heard or sensed him and stopped and turned. It still clutched at its arm and swayed a little, making groaning noises. The bulgy eyes were half closed in a grimace of pain – the too many teeth gleamed in the green gloom.

Mythil held the knife out like a sword. For a minute the spirit turned into a boy but he couldn't seem to keep that shape. He turned and began to limp and shuffle faster.

Mythil was elated. The tables were turned at last. Now the yaka was scared of him, he thought. He ran on after him, forgetting Ianthi, forgetting their worried, angry parents for the moment. He tripped on a root but regained his footing and tore after the yaka again. For a wounded creature, he could move fast, Mythil thought. He lost sight of him once or twice but kept on going. He got scratched by branches and tripped a couple of more times but hardly noticed, he was so intent on the chase.

And then a crash and a blood curdling scream stopped Mythil in his tracks.

What had happened now? He stood stock still. Had the yaka been attacked? What could make a yaka scream like that? The screaming turned to whimpering. Cautiously he made his way forward. Peering from behind a boulder Mythil caught his breath at what he saw. The yaka's leg was snared in a vicious-looking iron trap that must have been set for wild boar. His tummy did a little flop. He felt an imaginary ache in his own leg. The yaka was struggling in vain to open the jagged iron jaws of the trap and he felt unspeakably sorry for it. But how could a spirit be caught in an iron trap? Was it trying to trick him into thinking he was safe?

Then another thought struck him and he went cold. So there really were poachers in the jungle, he thought. Who else would have set a trap like that? Were they close by? Would they come for the sound of the trap shutting? Oh no – and what about Ianthi? Would they get her? With difficulty, he focused on the yaka again.

The creature looked up at Mythil and cowered, baring his long jagged teeth at the same time. Was it safe to approach the yaka, Mythil wondered. It certainly looked like the tree-spirit was well and truly snared. Taking a deep trembling breath, Mythil stepped forward.

Immediately the yaka lunged at him and Mythil sprang back with a yelp of fear. But the creature had fallen back again whimpering piteously.

He bared his teeth and made a ferocious growling noise but this time Mythil wasn't so scared. He is trapped, Mythil thought. Well and truly trapped. He took a few steps forward.

'I'm not going to hurt you,' Mythil said, 'unless you try to hurt me.' He brandished the knife and this time the yaka cowered back. 'Why did you attack me?' he asked wondering whether the creature was capable of speech.

He mumbled something. 'What?' Mythil asked.

'Only a bit of fun,' the creature whimpered. And when it looked at Mythil through tangled hair, Mythil saw a boy's face looking at him. A grimy, tousle-headed boy with tear-stained cheeks. 'Aaai, aaai, my leg,' the boy moaned.

'How do you do that?' Mythil asked taking a step back, bewildered by the sudden change. Seeing a snared yaka was one thing but seeing a wretched looking boy caught in the horrible jaws of the trap was quite another.

'Please set me free,' the boy said. 'I will do anything for you.'

Mythil had to remind himself that the boy was a yaka. He had seen its true face. 'Why should I trust you?' he asked. 'I know what you are. You are a tree spirit. Why can't you escape?'

'It hurts,' the boy said. 'The iron is hurting me and sapping my strength.'

'But it's not doing what it did earlier,' Mythil realised. 'There are no blue lights.' He looked at the penknife. Was it made of a different metal to the trap? Mythil remembered his comic books. Perhaps it worked like kryptonite for Superman and robbed the yakas of their power.

He brought the blade closer to the boy who groaned. Mythil noticed with surprise that a bright blue light was dancing along the silver blade. The knife must be made of some special kind of metal, he thought. A metal which sapped the spirits of their power much more powerfully than normal iron. The boy's eyes turned red and as Mythil watched him, he dissolved back into the spirit form.

'Don't hurt me. Please. Get away,' the spirit moaned. 'The pain. . . is. . . unbearable.'

Mythil took a few steps back. Having a weapon that was this powerful against the spirits was something he had never even dreamed of. But now that he had that kind of power he didn't feel elated. He actually felt quite sick. The yaka was obviously in terrible pain and he had caused it.

His legs suddenly felt wobbly and Mythil sat on the leaf-covered ground with a bump. The spirit stopped moaning and looked at him in what Mythil imagined to be surprise. It was difficult to read subtle expressions on its animal-like face. What should he do now? Could he set the yaka free and be sure that it wouldn't attack him? He glanced around at his surroundings for inspiration.

The path was almost invisible here and trees grew very close to each other. Mythil leaned against a tree-trunk and closed his eyes for a second to gather his wits together. He had to get as much information as he could from this yaka now before it got stronger and broke free of the trap he thought. Yes, that was the best thing to do. After that he would set it free.

He remembered Archchi's story about the robber. Her bluff had worked. Maybe he could try bluffing too. He decided to remain on the ground because he didn't trust his legs to hold him up.

'Right, I will let you go but first I want answers,' he said boldly, pointing the knife at the yaka and waving it for emphasis. The yaka stopped whining and seemed to look at Mythil expectantly. 'And if you don't give them to me, I will bring the knife to you again. Understand?' the yaka nodded.

'Okay, first question. Why did you attack me?'

The yaka shook his head. 'Just a bit of fun,' he repeated sniffling. Suddenly he didn't look all that scary to Mythil anymore.

'What do you mean fun? And why me? Why do you keep appearing to me every time I come to the jungle?' Mythil asked, a hint of anger in his voice. It was easy to pretend because he realised that he was a little angry. He had had a huge shock and now that it was wearing off he was beginning to feel impatient and irritable.

The creature shuddered and pulled against the trap that held it. Giving up, it too sat down with its injured leg stretched out in front of it. Mythil was glad there was no blood around the trap. The iron jaws seemed to have closed around the yaka's leg and held it fast.

'Ai. Poor, poor me. I just wanted a friend. For years I was a slave. Perhaps even centuries,' the yaka said. Gradually, as he spoke, he began taking on human features again. 'No will of my own. And then, and then I was granted freedom. After so long! But I used my freedom foolishly. On you.'

'On me?' Mythil asked, puzzled and apprehensive. Was the yaka trying to say that it was Mythil's own fault that he was seeing spirits? 'Go on. Start from the beginning,' he said in a bossy voice. 'How did you become a slave? And what do I have to do with anything?'

'We spirits have been on this land for thousands of years,' the yaka said hunching over and hugging itself. 'And some of us grew more powerful than others. The powerful ones will sometimes enslave the less powerful ones like me.

'Some let us go after the task is done. Or. . . or they absorb us so that our spirits merge into one and the powerful spirit becomes even more powerful,' the yaka said with another shudder. 'I don't remember who enslaved me or why or for how long exactly.' He was looking more like a boy now and Mythil could see that he was feeling very sorry for himself.

'How can you *not* remember?' he asked the yaka suspiciously.

'Whoever enslaved me must have made me forget,' the yaka said vaguely. 'Anyway, then I was free. I rushed around looking for a safe place. Away from powerful spirits who would want to make me a slave again. Then I found this little jungle. It was safe. So I moved in. There was no one so I was safe, you understand?'

'But it was also lonely. I had no one to talk to. For years and years. I was bored. Then you came. You were so scared!' The boy bared his teeth in a silent laugh that annoyed Mythil. 'You made the whole jungle tremble with your fear. You see, in the jungle if one creature is afraid everyone senses it and takes cover because they could also be in danger. You were scared of things you could not see. So I gave you something to see. Me.'

'Wait a minute, let me get this straight,' Mythil said half dazed by this information. '*You* gave me the power to see yakas?'

The boy gave another silent laugh and Mythil felt a tightening feeling in his chest. 'I gave you the power to see me in my true form. Humans don't have that power. If you see us, you only see us in our human form. Not our spirit form.'

Mythil's jaw dropped as this information sank in. His chest hurt and it felt like all the oxygen had been sucked out of the air. He took a ragged breath with difficulty. 'You gave me the power to see all yakas,' he said. And because of the tight feeling in his chest the words came out dangerously quiet.

The yaka boy blinked. 'No, no,' he said. 'I told you, I only gave you the power to see me.'

Mythil tried to breathe evenly. The stupid creature hadn't even realised what it had done.

'No. Not just you,' Mythil said through gritted teeth, 'I can see all the yakas in the world now thanks to you.' He shut his eyes and groaned. 'And you just did it for fun? Because you were bored?'

'But I didn't ...' the boy began to say, gaping at Mythil. But Mythil cut him off.

'You did this so you have to make it stop,' he said authoritatively. 'Make it stop right now.' Mythil was on his feet now and advancing on the yaka. The cold rage he felt surprised even him.

'Everyone thinks I am mad because of you! My parents are fighting because of you. They think I'm making up stories because they can't see you – only I can – and it's all your fault. Make it go away!'

A boon is a boon

The yaka cowered as Mythil advanced brandishing the knife. He kept morphing from boy to yaka now.

'I cannot! Please, you must believe me. I cannot. A boon is a boon. No one can take it back. That is the law.'

'What is a boon? And what law?' Mythil asked through gritted teeth holding the knife threateningly close.

'It is the law of the spirits,' the yaka gasped out as the blue lights began to dance on the knife blade again. 'When a spirit grants a boon – a gift you know – like your gift of seeing yakas. . .'

'It's not a gift,' Mythil interrupted, 'it's a curse! You've cursed me. My parents are already fighting because I'm seeing yakas. You've ruined everything!' Mythil yelled at the creature his face just inches away from its glowing eyes.

The yaka whined. 'Spare me. I am a good spirit. I'm not evil. I was lonely. How would you feel if you had no one to talk to at all. For years and years?'

Mythil paused for a moment. He *did* know what it was like to be lonely. The yaka noticed his hesitation. 'If we were friends I could help you,' he said earnestly. 'If we were friends you'd look out for me and I'd look out for you. That's what friends do, isn't it?'

Mythil recoiled. 'Be *your* friend? I don't want anything to do with you. You, you're a disgusting monster!' he said. 'You deserve to be left here in this trap until the poachers come and get you. Won't they be thrilled with their catch?' he said rather viciously.

He wasn't usually this mean but for the first time in his life Mythil was really scared. He was scared that this 'gift' of seeing yakas would only make things worse between his parents. He always tried to be well behaved when he was with them because he didn't want to give them a reason to start a fight. He didn't want Thaththi to tell Ammi that she had brought Mythil up badly. Nor did he want Ammi to tell Thaththi that any of Mythil's bad behaviour was because Thaththi was setting a bad example. So he always tried to be good. But if he was seeing yakas that no one else could see and his parents thought he was lying to get their attention, he was bound to be the cause of more fights. Mythil was so deep in his thoughts that he almost didn't hear the yaka's pleas.

'Set me free,' he was begging, 'and I will grant your every wish. I will. Just set me free!' the boy snivelled. He struggled to open the trap himself again but couldn't budge it.

Mythil dragged himself away from his worries. 'What do you mean you'll grant my every wish?' he asked puzzled. 'You said you can't take away this boon.'

A sudden hope sprang in Mythil's mind. 'Do you mean that even if you can't take away this boon you can grant me a different wish – I mean a boon? Another boon in return for setting you free?'

Now Mythil's mind was racing. Could he use the yaka like Aladdin's genie? If he asked for gold and jewels maybe his parents wouldn't need to fight about money all the time. Would that work? Would his parents stop fighting if they had enough money? He thought back to that afternoon's argument in front of Ianthi's parents. That hadn't been about money.

No – even if they had enough money they'd still fight about why I was seeing yakas, he thought. He had to stop seeing them. But how was he going to do that if the yaka couldn't take back his boon? He thought hard.

'Can you give me the power to choose when to see a yaka?' he asked the yaka eagerly. At least then he would be able to block them out when he didn't want to see them.

'Here, I don't have that kind of power!' the yaka said in alarm. 'If I was that powerful ...'

Mythil's hopes were dashed. 'You're such a little liar,' he told the yaka in disgust. 'You just said you could grant me any wish but you can't can you?'

'I am a poor, weak yaka. I have very little power,' the spirit said. Now his face was that of a boy's but the long gnarled hands he held up to fend

Mythil off were those of a tree-spirit.

'I am all alone. I need to save what little power I have left in case I need to hide from more powerful spirits. I have no family to protect me like you do. And now that I gave you a boon I have less power than before.' Mythil's upper lip curled in annoyance at this last comment but the yaka continued obliviously.

'If we were friends I could do all sorts of magic things for you. I would be very useful to you. I can be invisible and I'm one of the fastest messengers you ever saw. And it wouldn't matter if I had to use my power for these things because you'll be able to look out for me. I'd be safe from the other yakas until you die.'

'Until I die?' Mythil asked incredulously. This was one cheeky yaka, he thought. Did he honestly think that Mythil would save him from the other yakas let alone the iron trap after all the trouble he had caused? 'You don't want me to be your friend. You want to use me as a shield,' he accused the boy. 'They'll kill me to get at you!'

'That's not allowed,' the yaka said quickly. 'It's the law of the spirit-world. We cannot kill you. We can make your life miserable but we cannot take your life.'

'You're horrible,' Mythil said scowling at the messy, dirty creature that sat in front of him. 'You and all your spirit friends. I suppose you can make us go mad and kill ourselves if you wanted to.'

'Not me,' the yaka said earnestly. 'I don't have that kind of power. I'm all alone here and I need protection. Strong yakas, stronger than me can capture me if I have no power left.'

'You said there aren't any yakas here,' Mythil said scornfully. He was feeling dejected and let down. Yes, he had the yaka in his power but it was a weak, useless thing that couldn't help him.

'None living here, no, but they go around hunting for weak spirits like me. If they catch me they'll make me their slave, I tell you, or they'll absorb me.' Again the creature shuddered. 'And that'll be like death. This jungle isn't very big. If they thought of searching here they could easily find me.'

Even though Mythil was squatting close to the yaka he had let his knife hand drop to the ground and the spirit seemed to sense that it was no longer in danger. It went on talking. 'I tell you, they'd make me a slave again. And I will be made to do their bidding. Be my friend, take me home with you where it's safe and you will share my power.'

'No,' Mythil said getting to his feet. He looked at the yaka contemptuously. What an untrustworthy, deceitful thing it was. It didn't deserve to be set free to cause more trouble to humans.

'Why should I be your friend and take you home with me?' Mythil asked. 'So you can put me and my family in danger? No way. Because that's all that would happen, isn't it? You don't have any power. You said so yourself.'

'And if I take you in,' he went on, 'and there are dangerous spirits after you, they'll come after me and my family too. You can't make me stop seeing yakas and that's all I need right now.'

The yaka boy began sniffling again but Mythil pursed his lips in a thin line. 'I'm sorry but there's no way we can be friends. You're just trouble. All you care about is saving your own skin.'

And with that Mythil turned his back on the yaka and tried to walk away.

'Please, don't leave me here,' the yaka called out tremulously to Mythil. 'You promised to set me free if I spoke. I'll be at the mercy of the other yakas if you leave me like this. They'll kill me. Please! You have to let me go. I promise I'll stay out of your way if that's what you want. Please! You *said* you'd let me go.'

Mythil stopped with a sigh. Archchi always said a boy was only as good as his word. He hadn't exactly promised to let the creature go. But what would happen if he didn't? Would it be his fault if other yakas found him trapped here? He turned around and his eyes fell on the trap that had sunk its horrible jagged teeth into the spirit-boy's calf. Mythil supposed the iron had snagged the boy's spirit rather than actually broken bones – he wasn't human after all.

If he prised the trap open the yaka would be free to zip around the jungle again. Free to cause more havoc too, cast more spells on humans like him and turn their lives upside down.

'If I let you go will you leave this jungle and go far away and never come back?' Mythil asked. The yaka was tugging helplessly at the trap but he stopped at Mythil's words. A look of horror crossed his face.

'But where would I go?' he asked in a wailing voice. 'This is the only safe place I could find. And that was after searching and searching for so long ...'

Mythil raised his palm up wearily to stop the yaka from going on. Despite everything he had done that was annoying and just plain stupid, part of the reason he was caught in the trap was because Mythil had been chasing him. So if he did get caught by other yakas it would be my fault he decided.

He sighed, half annoyed with himself for being so weak. I should walk away, he told himself. Now that he had calmed down a little he knew that he couldn't just leave the yaka there like he had threatened earlier.

But was it really safe to let him go? He knew so little about this yaka. What evil was he capable of? Whose bidding had he done? 'Who were your masters before?' Mythil asked from where he stood.

The yaka stopped struggling with the trap. 'The memory of them has been wiped away,' he said whimpering because the iron hurt his hands. Mythil wasn't sure whether to believe him or not and the yaka seemed to sense it.

'It's true! I told you, they're powerful spirits. And I'm powerless against them. If they catch me ...' He let the sentence hang in mid air, sniffling and looking forlornly at Mythil as if to say 'only you can help me.'

Mythil remembered the old woman yaka. I guess she'd be a powerful yaka, he thought remembering that morning on the pavement outside Ianthi's house. *Ianthi!* Oh no. Where was she? She must be quite lost by now. What would the grown-ups say if he went back without her?

They don't believe there are yakas in the jungle, he thought in a panic, so they might think I deliberately let her get lost just to attract attention to myself. He groaned as he turned to the yaka.

'When you attacked me there was a girl with me. You know this forest. If I help you out of that trap can you find her? Can you take me to her?'

'In a flash!' The spirit said forgetting to snivel. Mythil was relieved. At least he wouldn't be in trouble about losing Ianthi he thought.

'But not now,' the yaka said dashing his hopes again. 'I need to wait till my strength comes back.'

'We don't have time,' Mythil told the yaka desperately. 'I need to find her and take her back now.'

He looked around and yelled, 'Ianthi! Can you hear me?' There was no reply. She wasn't even within hearing distance, he worried.

Then the yaka sniffed in Mythil's direction. 'Kevili! You have kevili,' he said sniffing out the 'bait' Mythil had brought with him to attract the yaka. 'If you give me some I will get a bit of power back. I can snap this trap and take you to the girl in moments.'

'And how do I know I can trust you?' Mythil asked tightening his grip on the penknife.

'It is the law of . . .'

'All right, all right,' Mythil said impatiently. 'It is the law of the spirits, right?'

'Yes, it is the law of the spirits. If you spare my life and give me food I am bound by the law to protect you and never hurt you.'

'Who made this law?' Mythil asked.

The yaka shrugged, his snub nose still twitching as he tried to sniff out the scent of kevili. 'It is written in my head.'

Great! Mythil thought sarcastically. Bad enough he was talking to a yaka – he was talking to one that had 'things' written in his head. Mythil pulled out the packet of kevili from his pocket and after hesitating a moment chucked it at the yaka. The creature grabbed at the paper bag parcel and tore it open with his claw-like hands, wolfing down the contents even before the bag was fully open.

Mythil stood ready to swipe at him with his knife if the creature attacked. How powerful could kevili make him, Mythil wondered. Perhaps I should have thrown him the sweetmeats one by one. That way I could've stopped before he got too powerful. Too late now.

Then a thought struck him. 'If you're a spirit – how can you eat?'

The yaka smacked his lips loudly and stretched. It was morphing completely into a boy once more. Gone was the tattered sarong he had been wearing before. Now he had on a very baggy, old fashioned pair of shorts.

'Eating doesn't give me any power. It's the act of giving that does. But eating is such a glorious thing isn't it? We spirits use up a little of our power just to enjoy the sensation of eating and tasting.'

The boy kicked out and the trap flew off his foot. It landed a few yards away. He grinned at Mythil.

'How will you find her?' Mythil asked, still keeping his penknife open and pointed at the yaka. 'She must be miles away from us by now.'

'Can't you feel her fear?' the boy asked, smiling gleefully. 'She is like you were the first time. She is making the jungle tremble with her fear. We just need to latch on to that.' He reached out towards Mythil but Mythil brandished the knife at him. 'You're going to have to trust me,' the yaka said.

'Well I don't,' Mythil said shortly. 'So don't even think of asking me to put the knife away. Any funny business and you get it in the arm again.'

The yaka laughed and disappeared. Mythil blinked. Where had the creature gone to?

Then Mythil felt a hand on his shoulder and before he could turn around he had the strangest sensation – like déjà vu, and the feeling that the trees had suddenly moved or changed. He realised that the trap that had been lying a few feet away was now missing. They had moved to a completely different part of the jungle.

A faint cry came to his ears. 'Mythil! Anybody! Help me!'

'That's Ianthi!' Mythil exclaimed moving towards the voice.

As good as his word

'Do you want me to disappear again?' the boy asked.

'Disappear?' Mythil asked swinging back towards him.

'She can't see me in my spirit form,' the yaka said, still grinning.

'She did. That's why she ran away . . .' Mythil began.

The boy let out a peel of laughter and sprang up into the branches of a nearby tree. 'She saw a boy jump out at her,' he said with a wide grin as he leapt down next to Mythil again. 'She was so scared of the jungle already that she just ran.'

'Hello? Anybody there?' Ianthi called out.

'Shhh!' Mythil admonished in a low voice. 'So you can't make her see your yaka shape?'

'I told you, I am not a powerful spirit. It takes a lot of power to show my yaka self to a human. That's why I granted you the gift of seeing me. Then even if I was weak after granting you that boon you'd still be able to see me. It's easier to be invisible or to take this boy form – though I cannot make it grow older like other yakas can.' He cocked his head to one side as though he was listening. 'Come on,' he told Mythil. 'Your friend is moving away.'

Mythil followed the yaka almost mechanically, deep in thought. 'So you've been in this jungle for years and years?' he asked. 'But if you can show your human form to people, why can't you make friends?'

'Before I was enslaved I used to befriend human families and help them work the land for a few years. That's how I collected power.' The boy leapt up into a wild siyambala tree and returned to Mythil's side with a handful of ripe fruits.

'Collect power? What do you mean?' Mythil asked taking a siyambala pod and snapping its shell with his fingers. Ianthi's voice was getting further away but he was confident now that the yaka could find her. Even though he was annoyed at him Mythil couldn't help feeling curious about the creature's world. That trick of moving from one place to another was certainly impressive.

'Well, as time passes we spirits get stronger if we don't use up our power,' the yaka said spitting out siyambala seeds before continuing. 'When I say "time" I mean centuries. That's why I'd become part of a family. They wouldn't know I was a yaka of course. And the power-hungry yakas stayed away from human settlements because they were afraid of the yakaduras – the exorcists. So I was usually safe.'

'You weren't afraid of the exorcists?' Mythil asked. He popped a siyambala into his mouth and sucked on the sour-sweet coating that covered its seeds.

'No, small-fry like me had nothing to fear from them.' To Mythil's surprise the yaka pulled out a catapult from his pocket. 'What an exorcist does when there is a troublesome yaka is to call on a more powerful yaka and ask it to chase the other one away. So I was safe in the villages. I didn't cause trouble and I wasn't powerful enough to be summoned by the yakaduras.'

Fitting a siyambala seed into the catapult the yaka shot it off into the trees overhead. 'See this catapult? I had to replace the strappy bit because it was falling to pieces but the wooden handle is just as it was when I first got it. It's made from a guava branch. It was a gift from one of my human friends so many, many years ago. They're probably long dead now.' The yaka shook himself and continued, 'Anyway, after a while I'd move on to another village, to another family somewhere else, when they began to wonder why I didn't grow up like their own children.'

'All that has changed now,' he sighed offering more siyambala to Mythil. Mythil shook his head and the yaka went on. 'It's difficult to find families who will take me in. That's why I was so lonely. Even though I can make my human form visible to people, I can't make friends. People aren't trusting like they used to be.'

He made a face. 'And then there are the officials who come around and ask all kinds of questions. Where are you from? Who are your parents?' He shot another black seed off into the branches with his catapult. 'And now I am afraid. What if some of these officials are powerful yakas in human form? They could be hunting us lesser spirits. To capture us and become more powerful.'

Like Aunty Nilmini, Mythil thought with a start. She works as a children's counsellor for charities around the island. Was she a yaka? Or maybe she was in league with the old woman yaka and she hunted out lesser spirits for the more powerful yakas, Mythil thought. He felt goosebumps popping up on his skin as he realised how cleverly deceptive Aunty Nilmini was – *if* his guess was right.

'That's why I was so bored. I had nowhere to go,' the yaka went on with his story. 'I was afraid to leave the jungle but so few people came here that it was dull. It's no fun being all alone and afraid all the time.'

Mythil felt a slight twinge of sympathy for the yaka. He had sometimes wished that he had a brother or sister to play with. It wasn't any fun being at home on your own when your parents were fighting, he thought. But he loved his parents too. Even when they fought like kids in front of strangers like Ianthi's parents. That thought brought him back to the present with a jolt.

'Ianthi!' he called out.

'Hello! Is anyone there? Help!' That was Ianthi again sounding further away.

'All right,' Mythil said making up his mind quickly and turning to the yaka. 'I want you to keep this boy form. I'm going to tell Ianthi that you're the one who scared us and you're going to take us home. The normal way. No magic, okay?'

The boy grinned, his eyes gleaming mischievously.

'Ianthi! Where are you?' Mythil called out, pushing through the thick undergrowth and trying to move towards her voice.

'Here! Mythil, I'm here!' her voice rang out joyfully. Mythil heard her crashing about close by.

'I'm over here,' he called out just as she burst out of a thicket and flung her arms around him. Mythil pulled away quickly. It was a reflex action. He felt shy and awkward again but strangely he thought that if she were to hug him again he probably wouldn't pull away.

'I was so scared!' Ianthi was saying. 'There were nasty branches everywhere and look – I've lost some of the sequins on my butterfly,' she said pointing to the white patches in the sequin-embroidered butterfly on her t-shirt.

Mythil felt bad for not having rescued her sooner. Her hair was all a mess with twigs and leaves stuck in it. Her elbows and knees were grubby and her sandals were caked with earth.

Then she saw the boy and flew at him with a scream. 'You! You're the one who jumped out and scared us! You animal! You rotten, rotten boy! I thought I was lost forever . . .'

'Hey, it's okay,' Mythil hurried to calm her down as the boy leapt out of her reach still grinning from ear to ear. 'He made a mistake. He was just fooling around and er... didn't think we'd get so scared. And he's very sorry. Aren't you?' Mythil asked the boy threateningly.

The boy nodded, 'Very sorry,' he said. But Mythil wished he would wipe that big fat grin off his face.

'Do you know him?' Ianthi asked Mythil as she brushed away at a grubby elbow.

'No. I've never er . . . seen his face before today.' Mythil said truthfully as he and the yaka exchanged fleeting glances. He looked at Ianthi's tear-stained face and wondered whether she would believe him if he told her that the boy was really a yaka. After all she was different from other girls. He was about to say something when she spoke.

'Can we go home now?' Ianthi said brushing at a leaf on her shoulder. 'I think I've had enough of this yaka game for today.'

Mythil clamped his lips together. Yaka game? No, maybe Ianthi wouldn't believe him either. He turned to the yaka. 'Take us back now. And take the quickest route.'

Still grinning the boy turned and pushed his way through the jungle. He had a pronounced limp but Mythil wasn't sure whether he was pretending or really hurt. He hadn't noticed the limp before. And anyway if he was a spirit, the yaka-boy couldn't have a limp, could he?

Mythil noticed the boy's catapult sticking out of his back pocket and a thought suddenly struck him. That first time when he had come to the jungle something had hit his ear. Could it have been a siyambala seed from the yaka's catapult? The more he thought about it the more certain Mythil was that that was what had struck his ear. The little louse, Mythil thought, feeling his irritation growing.

'How do you know he'll take us home?' Ianthi whispered as they scrambled through some prickly shrubs. The yaka held some of the branches back and Mythil helped Ianthi through.

'He's scared of me,' Mythil replied shortly. Ianthi looked sceptical so Mythil whispered in her ear, 'He thinks I'll really use this penknife – he's a bit slow.'

Even as he said the words Mythil felt the yaka's hand on his elbow and had that funny déjà vu feeling again. They'd just moved to another part of the jungle he realised in annoyance.

'Ooh, I feel dizzy,' Ianthi said leaning on Mythil.

'You've just had a bad scare,' Mythil said masking his growing irritation at the spirit boy and supporting Ianthi with his arm. 'You'll be all right in a moment.'

He glared at the yaka. I said no magic – he thought angrily. It was all very well for him to show off his magic in front of Ianthi but Mythil would be left to do all the explaining if she guessed something strange had happened. And as she couldn't see the yaka's real form she'd just think that he, Mythil, was mad when he tried to explain.

The boy's smile wavered slightly under Mythil's baleful stare but he called out gleefully. 'You're almost home! Listen, you can hear the stream.'

'Wow, were we that close to home?' Ianthi asked straightening up and letting go of Mythil's shoulder. 'I thought we must have been in the middle of the jungle – it felt like I was walking around for hours!'

'Perhaps you just walked in a circle and ended where you started,' Mythil said lamely as they came upon the stream. But Ianthi wasn't listening to him.

'What's your name?' she asked the boy. He smiled and offered her some siyambala but said nothing. 'Don't worry, I'm not going to get you into trouble,' she said taking one politely but looking like she didn't know what to do with it. 'Even though I should. You're the one who scared us and it's because of you we got lost.'

'You can call me Asiri,' the boy said with another beaming smile. He pushed the rest of the siyambala into her hands. 'Because I bring luck.'

Mythil snorted, but Ianthi smiled back at the boy. 'You did bring us back safely Asiri, and that was lucky for us. So we're willing to be your friends. Aren't we, Mythil?' she asked.

'No,' Mythil growled. He was still annoyed at the yaka for playing tricks on him. It seemed the spirit never learned, he thought. First this so-called boon which was ruining his life and now even after he had told the yaka no magic – he had used it to get them here. Used it in front of Ianthi too. And his ear still stung from yesterday, he told himself, from when he'd been hit quite viciously with a seed from the catapult.

'We should go back,' he told Ianthi. 'They'll be looking for us.' For the first time since they'd met her the boy completely lost his smile and looked sad. He fitted another siyambala seed into his catapult but didn't take aim.

Ianthi hung back. 'Do you want to come with us Asiri?' she asked. 'Have you had lunch?'

'I should go,' the boy said glancing at Mythil. He seemed at last to understand just how angry Mythil was with him.

Mythil turned away from them. He looked at the house across the stream and remembered the day before when Thaththi had driven off in a rage. He remembered his parent's arguments and how now he was the reason why they were fighting. No one believed he was seeing yakas and no one could help him stop this terrible curse. And it's all because of the yaka's stupidity, Mythil thought. He's a dishonest, untrustworthy, trickster spirit. He's the reason why everyone thinks I'm mad.

A steely look crept into Mythil's eyes. 'Yes, you should go. You'll get into trouble if Jamis finds you,' he said. 'Jamis is on the lookout for the boy who scared me and if he finds you . . .' Mythil broke off. Asiri had turned away and was walking back into the jungle.

'Come on,' Mythil said to Ianthi. 'Let's go home.' He knew she was looking at him reproachfully but he told himself that he didn't care. And anyway, even if Ianthi didn't know it, Mythil knew that Asiri was really a yaka. There was no way he was taking him home. He wished though that he could forget how sad Asiri had looked when he spoke of his search for a family.

How would he have felt if he didn't have a family to take care of him or anyone to talk to? Just one afternoon on his own had been bad enough. Years and years alone must be unbearable. But Mythil put those thoughts aside and hardened his heart. They weren't his problems, he told himself. He had enough worries of his own.

They crossed the stream after Ianthi had stopped to wash her face and arms in it. 'You've got leaves on your head,' Mythil said helping her to brush some of it out of her hair.

'I felt kind of sorry for him,' she said, adjusting her butterfly clip as they walked back. Anger and perhaps a little jealousy stirred in Mythil's heart. He didn't reply.

'Poor Asiri. I wonder whether he has a family. Doesn't look like anyone bothers to take care of him. I'm sure my mum could help find a home for him,' Ianthi went on. Mythil gave her a searching look but said nothing.

What if Aunty Nilmini was one of the spirit-finders as he suspected? What if her counselling was just a cover? All weak spirits could only take the form of children, he guessed. So her job was a perfect cover. Should he tell Ianthi not to tell her mother? If he was right and Ianthi told her mother about the boy she'd know for sure that there was a lone boy-spirit out there in the jungle.

On the other hand she hadn't seen the tree-spirit in the jungle when he was making faces at her earlier that afternoon. Even though she had been looking directly at the yaka on the tree. If her job was trapping spirits for other yakas, wouldn't she be able to see them? Unless she was pretending not to ...

Mythil's head hurt from thinking so much. What am I doing, he thought angrily. I don't care what happens to Asiri. I have my own problems. I'm not going to tell Ianthi not to tell her mother about the spirit-boy. What if I'm wrong and her mother isn't a yaka or a yaka-finder? Even if I'm right who would believe me, he thought bitterly. They'd just laugh at me or think I was looking for attention. So he said nothing.

Evening plans

'Well, we didn't find the yaka,' Ianthi said as they sat on the steps to the veranda. She was enjoying the ripe brown siyambala after Mythil had shown her how to crack open the shell.

It had felt like forever in the jungle but when Mythil and Ianthi had peeped in on their parents from one of the hall windows they had realised with relief that they hadn't been missed.

'What will you do now?'

Mythil shrugged. He was glad that the jungle adventure hadn't got him in trouble but he was still upset. Everything else was going wrong and there was nothing he could do about it. Sure, he had family to look after him unlike Asiri but what good were they when they didn't believe him, he thought gloomily.

Ianthi pulled out a few nails from her pocket. 'Too bad we never got to use these,' she said. They looked out at the jungle together from the veranda.

'Hey, what if we put these nails around the house?' Ianthi asked spitting out a few siyambala seeds on to the lawn. 'Then the yakas won't be able to get in because there'll be a ring of iron around the place. We could start from here. This rainwater drain runs right around the house doesn't it? We could drop the nails in there one by one.'

Mythil shrugged. 'Okay,' he said listlessly.

'And we've got to make sure no one sees us, right?' Ianthi asked.

'Especially Jamis.' Mythil said setting off around the front of the house.

His path took him past the hall and Ianthi's took her around the kitchen. By the time they met on the other side Mythil was feeling a little better. He still didn't have a clue how to fix his problems though. Maybe he could find and befriend another yaka. Now that he knew that yakas weren't allowed to kill humans and that some were friendly he had hope. And that was better than nothing.

'Done?' Ianthi asked as they met on the other side of the house.

'Done,' Mythil said.

'Anybody saw you?' Ianthi asked.

'No,' Mythil said. 'You?' Ianthi shook her head giving Mythil seven or eight left-over nails. He slipped them into his pocket.

'What's the plan now?' Ianthi asked. Before Mythil could reply a voice called out to them.

'Oh there you two are!' It was Aunty Nilmini. 'We have to go into town Ianthi – have to get your wound dressed you know!'

'Oh, Mummy, no! Not yet!' Ianthi wailed. 'Can't we do that later?'

'No, darling, we have to get your wound dressed today and Mythil's grandma says we can do it in town. It'll be too late by the time we get to Colombo.'

She smiled at Mythil but he didn't return the smile. He was staring intently at her, willing her to show him her yaka face. Nothing happened and Mythil's shoulders slumped in defeat. Perhaps she was just a regular aunty after all, he thought.

'But we'll be meeting again in the evening Mythil,' Aunty Nilmini said mistaking Mythil's unsmiling face for disappointment. 'There's a little museum in town and your parents have said that we can all meet together there later on and after that we'll go to the Rest House for dinner. Won't that be nice?'

Ianthi grinned at her mother and put her arm around her waist. 'It'll be late when we get back to Colombo but you can sleep in the car darling,' Aunty Nilmini told her daughter, brushing another small leaf off Ianthi's hair.

'I always fall asleep in the car,' Ianthi told Mythil. 'Even when I was a baby, if I couldn't sleep my parents would take me for a drive and I'd be asleep in no time.'

Mythil nodded but said nothing. 'What were you two playing at?' Aunty Nilmini asked brightly.

A mad desire came over Mythil. Did Aunty Nilmini think he was crazy? Did she think he saw imaginary yakas? All right, *let* her think that. 'We were fighting yakas in the jungle!' he said fiercely, brandishing a nail at her.

Aunty Nilmini recoiled in horror. 'Oh!' she said, catching her breath. 'What a rusty old nail! Careful you don't catch tetanus ...'

But, having got over his wild impulse, Mythil felt embarrassed. He jogged away in search of Archchi. She was on her way out from the pantry with her bottle of chutney and parcels of kevili.

'There's plenty left for you Mythil,' she told him with a wink. He felt a pang as he remembered his harsh words to her earlier. He reached out and carried as many packages as she would let him. They walked towards the car where the others had congregated.

'Thanks for driving all this way,' Thaththi was telling Uncle Anthony. Thaththi had his arm around Ammi and Mythil felt as though a load of boulders had rolled off his shoulders. They didn't look like they were mad at each other anymore.

'Yes, we appreciate what you're doing,' Ammi was saying. She broke off as Archchi and Mythil approached and helped hand the parcels over to Aunty Nilmini.

'My goodness, look at all these parcels!' Aunty Nilmini exclaimed, carefully placing them on the back seat as Archchi explained what was in each one. 'If they're half as good as that pudding they'll be gone before we get to Colombo!' she said.

Everyone laughed and Mythil felt a bit embarrassed about having brandished the nail at her. She couldn't be a yaka, could she? He had to be mistaken about that.

'I'll make you fresh pudding to take home with you this evening,' Archchi told Aunty Nilmini.

'We'll see you in the evening Mythil!' Aunty Nilmini said with a bright smile. 'And remember what I told you about facing your fears.' Mythil managed to hold his smile for the required duration of polite smiles. To hide the stiffening corners of his mouth he bent his head and noticed a cobweb on the hem of his t-shirt. He guessed that he must have picked that up from the shed. Archchi secretly got rid of the cobweb for him.

Uncle Anthony patted him on the shoulder and said he was sure Mythil would soon stop seeing demons. It reminded Mythil of the time he had mumps and the doctor said the lumps on his cheeks would soon go away.

'We'll give you time to finish at the doctor's and meet with your charity people,' Ammi said as the other family got into the car, 'Would five o'clock be a good time to meet up? I think the museum closes at six.'

'Oh that would be fine,' Aunty Nilmini said as the shutter rolled down automatically.

At last the long goodbye was over. Ianthi waved at them through the rear windscreen as the car rolled out along the drive and Archchi, Thaththi and Ammi waved back. When Mythil glanced at Ianthi as the car turned on to the lane she gave him another grin and the thumbs up sign. Then with a peeg-peeg the car sped off.

Who am I?

After the washing up was over his parents retreated to their room to chat and Mythil snuggled up in bed between them. He felt safe. If only it could always be like this. Ammi was telling Thaththi about how her father used to take her and her brothers to the museum when they were young.

'We really enjoyed those times because he could tell such great stories about every item on display,' Ammi said. 'I think that's why I got so interested in history. Perhaps you've inherited your vivid imagination from him Mythie-boy.'

She smiled and ruffled his hair. 'You know you can talk to us about anything, don't you Mythie?' she asked.

Mythil smiled even though it felt like the big boulders had rolled back on to his shoulders again. He remembered overhearing the grown-ups' conversation that afternoon and he knew he couldn't tell them about the yakas. His parents loved him and were worried about him but they just couldn't understand that the yakas were real.

What happens the next time I see a spirit like the old woman yaka, he wondered? Am I strong enough to fight it on my own without telling Ammi and Thaththi? Mythil sighed in frustration.

I need to find that yaka boy, Asiri, again and ask him whether one of the more powerful yakas might be able to help me to control what I see. If he says yes, the next time I meet a powerful yaka – I'll have to find a way to make it give me that boon. I'll have to face up to my fears as Aunty Nilmini said, Mythil thought grimly.

He waited till his parents were deep in conversation about something and then slipped out of bed, climbing over Thaththi's feet. 'Thirsty,' he said before anyone could ask him where he was going.

In the garden, making sure no one saw him, Mythil turned over the flowerpot where he had hidden the ornament, his small stash of nails and the penknife. Pocketing the knife and carefully hiding everything under the pot again he ran off towards the jungle.

When he got to the hollow tree all was quiet once more. Nothing stirred. He looked around carefully, knife out and on the ready. The yaka didn't seem to be around.

'Where are you?' he said forcefully. 'Show yourself!' For good measure he added, 'I have the knife with me.'

Something small fell on to a clump of tall grass. Mythil craned his neck but could see nothing. Something else, just as small, hit the grass and disappeared. Was the yaka-boy Asiri playing games with him again he wondered angrily. He seemed to be behind the banyan tree, on the other side of the rock. Mythil crept around the rock and leapt out brandishing his knife. But he was wrong.

Sitting at the foot of the tree, eating a papaw was a bare bodied little man with thick curly hair loosely gathered behind his neck and rippling down behind him. His skin was smooth and shiny and adorned with silver jewellery. He looked up at Mythil, wiping his mouth with the back of his hand.

'Ah, at last we meet him,' the little man said. He seemed to be talking to the papaw in his hand, Mythil thought, still dazed at this sudden apparition.

'Who are you?' Mythil asked cautiously. Surely this couldn't be another yaka? He took a step back and an overhanging banyan root hit the side of his face making him jump.

The little man peeled back the papaw skin and bit into the fruit. He had only a loin cloth around his waist, but the rest of him was covered in silver jewellery. A thick silver chain hung around his neck, large earrings covered his earlobes, and bracelets gleamed on both wrists. Mythil wondered wildly whether he was a rich poacher or robber king.

'Who am I? Hmmm. Well, that is a question everyone asks themselves isn't it? At some point or the other. It's a very good question of course.' He looked directly at Mythil for the first time. 'So you don't know the answer?' he smiled but Mythil stared blankly back at him.

'Shall we give him a hint?' the man asked the papaw. 'Hmm, let me see. Ah yes, here's a good one. I am usually abstemious,' he told Mythil with a chuckle. 'Yes, that is a good clue. You wouldn't usually find me eating.'

Mythil gripped the knife tightly. What did abstemious mean? Should he know this little man? He did look a little familiar. Where had he seen him before? Was he the yaka boy – Asiri – in disguise? Perhaps the tricky little yaka had lied about not being able to change shape. Mythil opened his mouth to ask but the man spoke first.

'I see he has the knife,' the man was speaking to the papaw again. 'But does he know who *he* is?' He bit into the ripe orange fruit again and then spoke to Mythil. 'Perhaps in answering this question it is easier to consider what one is not, is that not so? For instance, I am not your little yaka friend in disguise.'

'How did you know that was what I was thinking?' Mythil stammered. 'Anyway he's not my friend,' he added quickly. 'But . . . um, do you know where he is?'

The bahirawaya smiled wryly. 'Well, that is the other great mystery isn't it? Who are you, is the question that takes primacy. And then of course the next unassailable question is *where* are you. You have a sagacious mind my young friend.'

A *what* mind? Mythil felt a little impatient but at the same time he didn't want to be rude. He had no idea who the man was or what he was talking about. 'What is sag . . . sag . . . that word you used just now? And primacy and absteam . . . abstem . . . I don't know what they mean. Can you speak in normal language please?' he asked as politely as he could.

'Oh, but of course, of course,' the little man said looking quite dismayed. 'I do apologise my friend. I am a sententious old fossil . . .' He realised that Mythil was looking puzzled again and hurried to explain. 'I speak in a language that is not of this age.' He shook his head ruefully again, his silver accessories clinking together. 'Old habits die hard.'

All of a sudden the man began making a funny hissy noise and Mythil wondered in alarm whether he was choking. Then he relaxed. The man was chuckling. His shoulders shook as he tried to hold back his mirth. 'In fact old habits are harder to get rid of than your yakas, aren't they?' he asked his eyes twinkling.

'How do you know about the yakas?' Mythil was bewildered and suspicious at the same time. But the man had his mouth full and didn't reply. 'Anyway they can't attack me,' Mythil said fiercely, 'I have . . .'

The little man sobered down and his right eyebrow went up a couple of inches. 'A knife to kill a yaka?' he asked. Again he didn't look at Mythil. He seemed to be talking to the fruit in the watti. 'Now that would be a powerful knife indeed.'

'Yes,' Mythil said with more certainty than he felt. He wasn't sure exactly how efficient the knife would be against a hoard of supernatural beings. But he didn't want the man to know that. Just as Archchi's bluff had worked with the robber, he hoped he could also trick the man into believing that he, Mythil, was more powerful than he actually was.

'A yaka can't touch you if you have iron,' the boy said pluckily. 'And this knife is special. It's a special knife that can kill yakas.'

The man sighed and nodded. 'Yes, that is certainly a special knife,' he said, throwing away the papaw skins. As they hit the ground they withered, Mythil noticed in surprise.

'But do you feel safe with that knife?' He picked up a yellow plantain and talked to it. 'No, I don't think so either. He would not be here in my jungle looking for answers if he felt safe, would he?'

Mythil didn't know what to say to that. The little man was right. He really wasn't sure how safe he would be with just the knife. And what had the man meant when he said my jungle. Could he really own the entire jungle?

He certainly looked prosperous with all that silver on him. And even though he only wore a loin cloth like some farmers did, his skin didn't look as though he had been out in the fields in the sunshine. But if he was rich why was he helping himself to the fruits from Seeli's puja? Perhaps he was mad, Mythil thought. After all, he spoke to the fruit. No sane person did that.

Mythil realised that the man had been observing him too. 'Ah, you are looking at the offerings left for me. Slim pickings but I suppose I shouldn't complain. It could be worse.' He sniffed in Mythil's direction.

'You didn't bring any kevili did you? I smelt it on you the last time you were here. Such a delectable smell . . .' He sighed and shook his head at the peeled plantain muttering something that sounded like, 'I wish people would start bringing me kevili again.'

Mythil shrank back against the rock clutching at a gnarled root that protruded over it. He was not quite sure whether he should be alarmed by the stranger's comment or not. How could this funny creature have known about the kevili?

And then everything clicked into place – 'You – you're the bahirawaya,' Mythil exclaimed. Then he bit his tongue remembering that Seeli had said he wasn't supposed to use its real name. Would the creature possess him now? He had to keep talking to distract it.

'Is . . . is this rock where you live?' Mythil stammered. His legs felt all wobbly again and he was glad he could hang on to the banyan root for support.

The man looked harmless enough. He looked a lot like the carving on the rock – though a little bigger and full of life and colour. His head and tummy weren't exaggeratedly big as it was in the carving and he was altogether much skinnier than his image.

'Is that why there's a carving of you on it? Then . . . then you must have seen the tree-spirit. And you must know about the boon he gave me. Can you make him take it back?'

The bahirawaya's smile vanished. All of a sudden he looked very stern. Mythil's blood froze as he remembered that even human sacrifices were said to have been offered to him.

'When a spirit grants a boon no one else can take it back,' the man said stiffly. Then he got all apologetic again. 'But I am sorry – do you know the word boon?'

Mythil nodded, his heart sinking at this news. 'Isn't there any way at all to stop this boon?' he asked trying to hide his dismay. 'Will I go on seeing yakas everywhere?'

'The prospect makes you despair. Quite understandable,' the man said sympathetically. Then he raised an eyebrow again. 'Oh but I am sorry – despair – do you know the word? It means to be upset, sad . . .'

'Yes, I know,' Mythil said through gritted teeth. Of course he knew what despair meant! He wasn't three years old. Was the bahirawaya making fun of him? Why did they not take him seriously – these spirits? They were all fooling around with him or trying to scare him – this bahirawaya man, that tree spirit and that horrible old woman yaka.

Mythil felt as though he was being bullied. His frustration helped him overcome his fear. 'I'm fed up of this. Everything is suddenly a nightmare. Everywhere I turn I see a yaka,' he said.

'Yes, that is certainly less than ideal,' the man admitted thoughtfully. He sighed. 'But then life is not always perfect, is it? I am a bahirawa lord and you may think that is an illustrious . . .' He threw a guilty look at Mythil again before continuing. 'Er . . . majestic, grand title. And it is. Quite so. But at the same time I am no more than a serf . . .'

'A smurf?' Mythil asked in surprise.

'Er . . . smurf? No, I am not aware of that word,' the bahirawaya said frowning and sounding puzzled. 'A smurf you say?' He pronounced the word as though it had an odd taste to it. 'No, I said I was like a serf. Er . . . you understand what a serf is? No?' Mythil shook his head. He knew that surf meant a wave in the sea but he didn't think that was what the bahirawaya was talking about.

'Oh well, I suppose it was long before your time. Yes. Long before your time a serf was known as someone who was bound to work the land for as long as he lived, no matter who owned it,' the bahirawaya said sounding happy to be talking about something he knew. 'And like a serf I am bound to my duties. Yes, serf, that's my middle name,' he chuckled to himself and glanced at Mythil to see if he thought that was funny too.

Mythil looked back at him stony-faced and the man stopped chuckling in a hurry. 'And of course when we look at your problem,' he said, as if rushing to assure Mythil that he really was concerned about Mythil's problem even though he had just been chuckling, 'it is quite troubling as well. Quite troubling. Yes, and the yakas have noticed your boon . . . er . . . your gift, haven't they?' he asked pursing his lips and shaking his head. 'Perhaps they will do something about it by and by.'

'Do something?' Mythil was startled. 'What? What do you mean?' he whispered still gripping the banyan root tightly, 'Please, tell me how I can get rid of this . . . this boon. Please, you must know a way.'

The man sighed. 'There was a time when I might have been able to help you. But now my powers have waned. I appreciate the pujas though.' He looked broodingly at the ground and then shook himself.

'Only you can help yourself. It was wrong of that mischievous tree spirit to grant you a boon the way he did. But even if there was a spirit powerful enough to bestow another boon upon you, would you bargain with it? Ah, then I would have to say temerity thy name is Mythil.' The man paused as though that was the punch-line of a great joke.

But Mythil wasn't laughing. He had no idea what that last sentence meant but it unnerved him to realise that the bahirawaya knew his name. The little man sighed. 'What would you give it in return?' he continued. 'Would you battle with it? Do you have any powers of your own?' the man asked.

Mythil shook his head.

'So what option do you choose when neither suits you?' The bahirawaya held a coconut in one hand and a mango in the other. 'You have to balance your choices and decide which one is better to live with.' He glanced at Mythil with a look that was curiously compassionate.

'I have listened to people telling me their worries over time Mythil. And it has been a long, long time,' the bahirawaya said almost dreamily. 'If there is one constant, it is that everything is always changing.' He brooded for a few minutes and then he seemed to snap out of it. 'So you might as well get used to it,' he said nodding solemnly at the coconut.

'You'll find that sometimes the changes are gradual.' He now held the coconut in both hands and began slowly raising it as high as he could reach.

'And sometimes they happen in an instant!' He brought the coconut down on to a stone with a crash, and as it split open, he disappeared.

'The trick is to adapt . . .' His voice grew fainter until it may have been just the whisper of the trees. 'Like the yakas did.'

Asiri's story

'Where are you?' Mythil called out. 'Serf?' But no one answered him. He scrambled around to the other side of the rock but there was no one there either. The jungle was quiet. What had the bahirawaya meant by saying that the yakas had adapted? And that they would do something about him? Was it a warning?

He was inclined to think kindly of the bahirawaya. There didn't seem to be anything to fear – the bahirawaya himself had said his powers weren't so great any more. So that just left the yakas as the most powerful spirits.

But I still don't know how to get the boon that will give me control over seeing the yakas, he thought. Mythil groaned out loud. Now what?

He shut his eyes and with clenched fists, willed the yaka-boy to appear. He opened his eyes but the clearing was empty. Again he shut his eyes and thought of everything that was worrying him. His parents, his boon and the yakas. He thought about them until his head hurt. If he could get agitated enough to make the jungle tremble, he may be able to attract the yaka, he thought.

He opened his eyes and called out, 'Yaka show yourself.' Nothing happened. Dejectedly he turned to leave. Then a twig snapped and a figure stepped out from behind a tree. It was Asiri. He was still in his baggy shorts but this time his hair was no longer tangled and he had on a t-shirt similar to Mythil's.

'You have no power to summon me,' the boy said. He wasn't smiling.

'But I have the knife and you know I will use it if you try any funny business,' Mythil warned. 'I just want to talk. You said you had no one to talk to.'

The boy sat down cross-legged on the ground and Mythil cautiously did the same, still gripping the knife. 'So talk,' Asiri said.

'You said there weren't any other yakas in this jungle. Do you know where

I could find one more powerful than you?'

'Ah, you need my help,' Asiri said a little mockingly. 'That's the only reason why you will have anything to do with me. Did you bring any kevili?' As he spoke his eyes began to glow.

'Stop that!' Mythil ordered.

'I'm not doing anything,' Asiri said. 'You're the one who's making me turn back into a yaka.'

'So you mean that when I see a yaka,' Mythil said, 'I make them change into their real forms and they know I can see them?' The bahirawaya had said that too – that the yakas had sensed his power to see them.

The boy nodded. He now had a yaka face but the rest of him looked human. 'When you look at me you make my yaka face appear. I can fight against your power and keep my human form but it takes a lot of energy. And I ...'

'You don't have a lot of power. You told me that before,' Mythil said impatiently.

'Yes, I don't have a lot of power so if they find me they will swallow me whole and make me do their bidding. Perhaps things I wouldn't want to do,' Asiri said, 'Like drive poor innocent people mad or ...'

Mythil heaved a big sigh and rolled his eyes before interrupting. This yaka loved to be dramatic, he thought. 'Because you can't take back the boon you gave me, the boon I need to get now is one that will give me more control,' he said. 'So that I can only see a yaka when I want to and in a way that they don't know I can see them.'

'Well, as I told you even if I had the power to give you that boon – and I don't – it would make me very, very weak. I would be just a yaka form without any power. I wouldn't be able to take human form or move from place to place. I would have nothing to bargain with and no protection. What human would make friends with me then? They wouldn't even be able to see me.' Asiri said all this a little defensively.

'That's why I need to find a more powerful yaka than you,' Mythil retorted. 'Serf doesn't think it's wise to make a deal with a yaka ...'

'Serf?' The boy interrupted. 'Who's that?' Mythil pointed at the carving on the rock. 'Is that your name for the banyan tree?' Asiri asked a little sarcastically.

'No,' Mythil said icily, 'It's my name for the person who is carved on the rock.'

Asiri leapt to his feet looking horrified. 'You're making fun of me,' he said turning into his yaka form completely and snarling at Mythil.

'I'm not,' Mythil protested. 'Why are you so scared of him?'

'The bahirawa lord is one of the most powerful spirits,' he said, staring at the rock carving as though he expected it to come alive and attack him. Mythil noticed that he was slowly regaining his human features.

'Well you can relax,' he said. 'His powers aren't great anymore.'

'What do you mean?' Asiri whispered. He still looked scared.

'Sit down,' Mythil said. 'Serf said he used to be powerful a long time ago, but now his powers have waned.'

'How?' Asiri asked finally sitting down. 'And why do you keep calling him Serf? That can't be his name.'

Mythil shrugged. 'I don't know how he lost his powers. All I know is he said his middle name is Serf. Was he supposed to be more powerful than the yakas?'

The boy nodded. 'From the beginning of time the yakas have always been afraid of the power of the bahirawa lords.'

'Lords? You mean there are more than one of them?' Mythil asked, fear creeping up his spine. What if there were other powerful spirits in the jungle? Asiri obviously couldn't detect their presence – he hadn't even known that the bahirawaya still lived in the rock. Or had he?

'But you must have known there was a bahirawaya here?' Mythil asked. 'You must have seen the carving on the rock before.'

'This was the first place I came to when I entered the jungle,' Asiri said still staring at the rock. 'I asked him for permission to seek refuge in his domain but I got no reply. I thought perhaps he had left.'

'Why would he leave?' Mythil asked, puzzled.

'They're all leaving,' Asiri said with a shrug. 'Maybe because your kind are destroying the jungles. Even this jungle is much smaller than it used to be so I thought he must have left too. I thought other spirits were staying clear of this area because they thought he was still here. I thought I was the only one who knew he wasn't here. Now you say he is. But his power is gone?' Asiri shook his head trying to understand how that could be.

'Do you think his power is connected to the jungle?' Mythil asked swiping away a mosquito that buzzed too near his ear. 'So because this jungle is much smaller than it used to be his power is less?'

Asiri made a don't-know-sign with his hands. 'The bahirawa lords' power is connected with the earth,' he said. 'But maybe the earth has to be covered in trees for him to get his power.' He stopped speaking and Mythil realised that there wasn't a trace of yaka on him anymore.

'How come you look fully human now?' he asked Asiri looking critically at the boy's features.

Asiri looked down at his hands in surprise. 'You're right. I'm not fighting your power anymore,' he said touching his face. 'Perhaps after the first glimpse you stop seeing us in our yaka form. That's good news, isn't it?' he grinned at Mythil jubilantly.

Mythil shook his head. How could Asiri sound so glib about everything? No, not everything – when it was something that threatened him, like the bahirawaya, he took it very seriously but if it was something that affected Mythil he seemed not to care at all.

'You still don't understand, do you?' he asked irritably. 'One glimpse is all they need to know I'm on to them. After that, I'm a target. They know I have this power and the only way they can stop me is to destroy me.'

Saying the words made him despair. He ran his fingers through his hair, tugging at a fistful in frustration. How could he fight a horde of yakas with just a penknife?

'Don't you know anyone who can take this boon away or give me the power to control it?' he asked Asiri half pleadingly. The other boy looked stricken.

'I never meant for you to be in harm's way,' Asiri said leaning forward and peering at Mythil earnestly. 'From the day I entered your world I have never hurt a human. I am a good yaka.'

Mythil sighed. He could see that it was useless expecting Asiri to know any powerful yakas. He had spent his entire existence on earth trying to avoid them. '*Where* do you come from?' Mythil asked picking up a twig and flicking a dry leaf off it. This was something he had wanted to know for a while now.

'The memories of where we came from and how we got here are very hazy,' Asiri said staring into space as he tried to recall. 'I seem to remember that we came out of a world of chaos. It seemed better here than where we came from so we stayed.'

'And just like that you and your kind took over our world,' Mythil said. He felt irritated. 'It's just not fair. You give me a boon that you don't have the power to take back and you don't even know anyone powerful enough to give me some control over it. I wish you'd just go back to where you came from.'

Asiri shook his head sadly. 'Even if I wanted to I wouldn't know how. And I am scared of what I will find there. Though I am all alone right now this world is my home. I've been living here for centuries now. I know how to live with humans and I haven't given up hope that I will find a friend or a family who will take me in some day.'

'Oh stop hinting!' Mythil said impatiently. 'Do you really think you know humans? Do you think you can come around, put my life in danger, and probably my family's lives too and then expect me to say "Right then, I love the way you're ruining my life. Why don't you be my friend?"'

Asiri grinned. 'You're funny,' he said.

'No, I am not!' Mythil snapped. 'Nothing is funny okay? It's dead serious. My life is in danger and it's because of you. You think you know so much about us – but you know nothing. I wish you'd never come here.'

Mythil buried his face in his hands and squeezed his eyes shut. 'There has to be a way to stop your kind.' He hit his knee with a clenched fist. 'And I will find it somehow,' he said fiercely.

'Let me help you,' Asiri said leaning forward and putting his hand on Mythil's shoulder.

'You can't help me,' Mythil said shrugging off Asiri's hand and standing up abruptly. 'Look, I know you're in trouble too but I can't help you okay? Go find someone else. I have enough problems of my own.'

With that he turned and walked away leaving Asiri sitting hunched up on the floor of the jungle in the gathering gloom.

The surprise

When Mythil got back there was an angry delegation waiting for him. Jamis the gardener had found the nails that he and Ianthi had put into the rainwater drain.

'If no one had seen it before the rains it would have clogged the entire system,' Jamis told Archchi, his lips set in a sullen curve and his grey eyes looking very angry. 'It was a good thing I found them when I did.'

'Did you put the nails in the drain Mythie?' Archchi asked with a look that seemed to say – now why would you do something like that?

Mythil nodded but didn't volunteer an explanation. He knew Jamis was getting back at him for their argument earlier on. He wasn't going to tell them it was Ianthi's idea and give the old gardener the satisfaction of hearing her being criticised too.

'All right Jamis, put the nails in a box and tomorrow Podi Baby will sort them out,' Archchi said with a sigh.

'It's a good thing I found them,' Jamis said shaking the nails that he had collected in a tin. 'There's going to be a storm later tonight.'

He kept muttering to himself, obviously upset that Archchi hadn't given Mythil more of a scolding. He seemed reluctant to leave. Mythil felt like sticking his tongue out at the old man but thought that that might be going too far.

Besides he knew Jamis was right – the nails would have clogged up the entire drainage system and that would have been a mess. Being so near to the stream Mythil knew how important it was for the drains around Archchi's house to be clear. Why hadn't he thought of that before agreeing to drop the nails into them with Ianthi, he wondered. My head was so full of yakas that I wasn't thinking straight, he thought.

'Yes, it is a good thing you found the nails before the storm,' Archchi told Jamis. 'Make sure the firewood is properly covered – I think this is going to be a big storm.'

The old man walked away reluctantly. Mythil followed Archchi inside glad that his parents weren't around. 'Why did you do such a childish thing Mythie?' Archchi asked when they were alone in the pantry.

'Iron protects against yakas, Archchi,' Mythil said tonelessly.

Archchi sighed. 'Yes, they say you can use iron to fight yakas. But you can also use your brains to fight them. And between you and me, I think you stand a much better chance using your brains. Now run along and get ready. Your Ammi and Thaththi are already getting dressed for the evening at the museum.'

Mythil was pre-occupied as he had a wash and changed. He wore a pair of dark blue trousers and an orange t-shirt that Archchi had bought him for his last birthday. Ammi had to send him back and make him wear his sandals and brush his hair when he absentmindedly got into the car without doing either. Archchi had made a fresh wattakka pudding to be given to Aunty Nilmini but she declined to go with them.

'You don't need an old lady slowing you down,' she told them. 'Enjoy your evening. I've had enough excitement for a day.'

So Ammi, Thaththi and Mythil set off without her. Ammi had changed into a pretty creamy-white dress with a pattern of tiny red flowers and green leaves. Thaththi wore jeans and a green t-shirt.

They drove past the village heading towards the town. Mythil was imagining what it would be like to walk into a shop and see a yaka. Perhaps if he didn't make eye contact they wouldn't change their shape and so they wouldn't know he could see them for what they really were.

As they drove past the doctor's Thaththi pointed out Uncle Anthony's car. 'They probably haven't finished with the doctor yet,' he said. 'After I check emails we can go and look for them.'

Then as they were passing the market Mythil spotted a familiar figure. Was it . . . could it be Aunty Bhishani – the old woman yaka he had met at Ianthi's? Whoever it was, the old woman was certainly wearing the same grey and white saree that Aunty Bhishani had been wearing that morning.

Mythil knelt on his seat to peer through the rear windscreen. He thought she was speaking with two men. But it was getting dark and the car was travelling too fast for him to see properly. The threesome was soon out of sight.

Mythil turned around to speak to his parents but they were preoccupied with a cow and her calf who couldn't decide which side of the road they wanted to be on. Mythil remembered his promise to himself not to tell them anything about the yakas and pursed his mouth determinedly. He had to solve this on his own.

They parked beside the newly built communication centre. Ammi said she would wait for them in the car so Thaththi and Mythil walked inside. The air-conditioned interior held little booths with computers and Thaththi found a vacant station. He and Mythil sat on two office chairs with wheels on them.

'Do you want to check anything on the internet for a few minutes when I'm done?' Thaththi asked Mythil.

Mythil's eyes lit up. Surfing the internet cost money and Thaththi didn't often let him do it unless he had a homework assignment or something important like that. An idea struck him. 'Do you think the internet will have anything on yakas and bahirawayas?'

'Probably not,' Thaththi said shortly. He looked like he was about to say something sharp about Mythil's fascination with yakas but then his emails started downloading and he lost interest.

Mythil was quiet while Thaththi ran his eyes down the list of new emails in the in-box. He kicked off his sandals and glided backwards till the chair hit the wall with a soft thump. Then he kicked himself forward, careful not to knock into Thaththi or jostle the table. He did this a few times making a mental list of the words he would use in the search engine to find out more about the yakas.

Then he saw Thaththi stiffen and click open an email. He glided closer and looked over Thaththi's shoulder. The subject said 'Application for Post of Technical Writer.' The email was addressed to Thaththi and started: "I have just gone through your writing samples and résumé and was very impressed. You seem to be just the person we are looking for . . ."

But before Mythil could read any further Thaththi had leapt to his feet, heaved Mythil up and swung him around. They crashed into Mythil's chair, but Thaththi didn't seem to care that he was getting odd looks from the other people.

He logged off and hurried to the counter, pulling out his wallet and dumping money on the table with trembling fingers. 'My print-out,' he told the man behind the counter. He drummed his fingers impatiently until the paper was given to him. Glancing at its contents once more Thaththi grinned and rushed out onto the pavement. Mythil hurried out after him. Thaththi seemed to have forgotten him.

Mythil scrambled into the car to find out what his father was so excited about. Thaththi handed Ammi the printout with a flourish. She read through it quickly. Thaththi turned and winked at Mythil.

'You got the job!' Ammi exclaimed. 'Mythil, Thaththi's got the job!'

'What job?' Mythil asked.

'I am pleased to inform you Mythil,' Thaththi said playfully, 'that your father has been accepted for a job in Hong Kong!'

'Hong Kong!' Mythil gasped.

'Oh yes, Mythie-boy! We're going to see the bright lights and sky-scrapers of Hong Kong!' Thaththi was beaming. Mythil couldn't remember seeing his father looking so pleased before.

'When do they want you to start?' Ammi asked reading through the letter again.

'I guess it's up to me to say,' Thaththi said. 'They're asking how soon I can join.'

'I knew something would work out,' Ammi said with a big smile of relief. 'We just had to be patient.'

'Let's not get ahead of ourselves now,' Thaththi said starting the car and pulling away from the curb. 'A lot of things have to fall into place first. Let's see what they're offering.'

'You're going in the wrong direction,' Ammi reminded him. 'We're meeting Nilmini and them, remember?'

'Ah! I forgot,' Thaththi said doing a u-turn. They drove past the doctor's but Uncle Anthony's car was no longer parked there. 'They must have headed for the museum already.' Thaththi said.

'How do you know Aunty Nilmini?' Mythil asked sitting forward and draping his arms around his parents' seats.

'Well, when we were children, or when I was a child – Nilmini was a good deal older to me – we used to live in the same neighbourhood. We were family friends, I guess you could say.'

So that means Aunty Nilmini is either a very powerful yaka who can make her human form grow older or she's just a normal human being, Mythil thought.

'But how do you know her now?' Mythil asked. He kept a lookout for Aunty Bhishani – had he really seen her?

'There they are,' Thaththi said as they turned down a short lane that led up to an old white building. Uncle Anthony's car was parked near the entrance.

He continued his story, 'I tracked her down when I applied for this job in Hong Kong. I knew she and Anthony had spent some years there and I was hoping they could give me some advice on getting a job.'

Aunty Nilmini had seen them and came down the flight of steps all smiles. Could she have been meeting with Aunty Bhishani at the market, Mythil wondered. 'Perfect timing,' she called out. 'We just got here too.'

Mythil noticed that her yellow skirt was now dry where it had got wet in the stream. Ianthi skipped down the steps of the building behind her mother. Her knees and the hems of her shorts looked a bit grubby from the afternoon's jungle excursion but her short hair had been brushed free of twigs and leaves and clipped back from her face with the blue butterfly clip.

'We've got good news, Nilmini,' Thaththi called out as he shut and locked the car door. 'I got the Hong Kong job!'

'Oh, that's fantastic, no!' Aunty Nilmini said beaming. 'Anthony will be so pleased. Let's go inside and tell him.'

'Here are the tickets!' Ianthi said giving Mythil a ticket to the museum.

'How's the wounded soldier?' Thaththi asked Ianthi as she gave him his ticket. She grinned at him.

'Fine, thank you. The doctor says I'll be okay with just a sticking plaster now. See?'

But Mythil was focusing on Aunty Nilmini. He was still wondering whether she could have met Aunty Bhishani at the market.

'I thought I saw you talking with some people when we drove past the market earlier,' Mythil bluffed – he hadn't seen Aunty Nilmini of course but if Aunty Bhishani was in town and Aunty Nilmini was helping her find lesser spirits she may have met the other yakas in town. Thaththi and Ammi looked at him in surprise but he monitored Aunty Nilmini's face carefully.

'Oh, that must have been when I met up with the people in my association. My word, look at the sky!' she said changing the subject and heading up the steps to the museum. Mythil couldn't decide whether she had been surprised by his comment. 'Looks like there's going to be a storm tonight! Let's go inside. Anthony's already looking around. And we have a surprise for you Mythil.'

They entered the gloomy interior of the museum and Mythil wondered what the surprise could be. He half hoped for a neek-neek toy though he knew that even if they could afford one for Ianthi they weren't likely to give him one.

The museum had been an old Dutch house built with thick white walls and columns, a red cement floor and a red tiled roof. Mythil and his parents handed in their tickets at the entrance corridor and walked into the main hall. And there to Mythil's horror and dismay, was Aunty Bhishani coming to meet them with Uncle Anthony.

In the museum

After the initial horror of seeing her there Mythil was filled with anger at his parents. *How* could they not have told him she would be there? *How* could they have agreed to have anything to do with her?

But he soon realised that they knew nothing about it when Aunty Nilmini said, 'Now I have a confession to make. I asked Bhishani to close the shop this morning and be here by this evening as soon as we decided to drive down here ourselves. I thought the best thing would be for Mythil to face his fears and see that she's just a normal old lady.'

As Uncle Anthony and Aunty Bhishani walked up to them she said, 'You've already met, haven't you?' beaming at Thaththi and Mythil. Mythil looked down at his sandals. Then he felt Thaththi's hand on his shoulder and was pleasantly surprised when Thaththi said, 'We have,' shortly, not bothering to hide the fact that he was annoyed. Mythil felt better.

He stole a look at Aunty Bhishani. She didn't look that fearsome. She was mopping her forehead with her handkerchief and fanning herself with the end of her saree pota, smiling and nodding at Ammi. He looked down at his sandals again before she could look at him.

'Nilmini, can we have a word with you please?' Thaththi asked crossing his arms.

Aunty Nilmini motioned to Uncle Anthony with her eyes and he took the hint. 'Come along, Ianthi,' Uncle Anthony said, putting an arm around his daughter's shoulder. 'Aunty Bhishani and I were looking at some interesting ancient clothes in this area.'

He, Ianthi and Aunty Bhishani moved away into the large, cavernous hall which housed large glass display cabinets with mouldy-looking clothes. Along the centre of the hall were glass-topped tables displaying maps. From the wooden beams of the roof hung an array of unpolished brass and metal lamps, some of them lit by electric bulbs.

Aunty Nilmini moved into a nearby ante-room with Ammi and Thaththi and they started talking in low voices. Mythil edged closer towards the door so that he could hear what they were saying. The room was quite small and held showcases of weights and measures and coins. He heard Thaththi say: 'I don't agree with you Nilmini. You could have told us . . .'

Aunty Nilmini interrupted, speaking in a low urgent voice. 'But it is all in his mind – the best way for him to overcome these fears is to face them and to start believing in himself . . .'

Mythil peered through the gap between the lintel and the door as Thaththi interrupted her. 'Look, I don't know what happened at your shop this morning but I heard enough from Mythil to know that that woman tried to hurt him or threaten him. You can't suddenly bring them face to face . . . I mean, isn't that irresponsible and drastic?' He looked very fierce and Mythil felt glad that he had a father who would fight for him even if he didn't believe that his son was seeing yakas.

'Oh, be reasonable . . .' Aunty Nilmini's voice was getting a little louder. Her eyes and her gold-hoop earrings flashed in the yellow light of the old-fashioned lamps.

'Hi?' Ianthi made Mythil jump. She had appeared from a nearby doorway. 'There's a weapons room through that door. Want to check it out?' The remaining sequins on her t-shirt glimmered in the lamplight.

Mythil scowled at her. 'As if I want anything to do with you!' he said fiercely, but keeping his voice down. Ianthi looked shocked. 'You were in on this plan too, weren't you?' he asked.

'You're not making any sense,' Ianthi said indignantly.

Mythil could feel Aunty Bhishani's eyes on them from the other side of the hall. Uncle Anthony was speaking to her about a map but she wasn't responding in any way and Mythil knew that she was straining to hear his conversation with Ianthi. So he moved sideways into the weapons room.

'You don't believe Aunty Bhishani is a yaka, do you? If you did you wouldn't have come here with her. If you believed that I really did see her yaka face you wouldn't want to be in the same room as her. You never really believed me, did you?'

'Mythil, I believe that you saw her face turning into a yaka face,' Ianthi said earnestly. 'I really do. But that doesn't *mean* that she's a yaka.'

'What do you mean?' Mythil asked exasperated by this statement. 'Do you believe I saw her as a yaka or don't you?'

'I've known her since I was a baby,' Ianthi said. Mythil remembered what the boy-yaka had said about the families he used to befriend. They never knew he was a yaka either. 'She's never been anything but normal.'

'So you think I'm mad?' Mythil asked bitterly. He turned away from her terribly disappointed. He had thought she was his friend.

'Nobody thinks you're mad,' Ianthi said soothingly. 'My mother says you're seeing demons because your parents are getting divorced and you don't want to face up to it.'

'Divorced?' Mythil could hardly believe his ears. 'They're *not* getting divorced! And they have nothing to do with the yakas!'

Ianthi looked unsure for a minute. 'But Mummy says it's only a matter of time before they . . .'

'Your mother is a yaka too,' Mythil spat out.

'My mother is a yaka?' Ianthi asked incredulously. 'Now you're really bonkers.'

'She left you and your father at the doctor's and went out didn't she?' Mythil asked accusingly.

'What does that have to do with anything?' Ianthi asked sounding irritated now. 'She was meeting those people from her children's charity.'

'She was with your precious Aunty Bhishani and the other yakas in town!'

Ianthi laughed and the angry tone left her voice. 'Mythil, I told you. She's not a yaka and neither is my mother. Aunty Bhishani's an old family friend. She's worried about you too. We all are.'

'But you don't think I saw the yakas,' Mythil said seething inside at Ianthi's patronising tone. 'You lied when you said you believed me!'

'I didn't lie,' Ianthi said heatedly. 'To you the yakas are real and I believe you actually did see them. That's why I played along with you. My mother's a great children's counsellor . . .'

'Oh really? What does she do exactly?' Mythil cut in sarcastically. 'She tells the kids they're mad and locks them up right?'

'Of course not,' Ianthi said sharply. 'She works with children who're troubled like you or who've been abused or abandoned and she helps them to integrate into society.'

Mythil wasn't exactly sure what integrate meant but in his mind's eye he could see Aunty Nilmini cornering child yakas like Asiri and saying, 'So you think you're seeing yakas do you? Now, don't run away. You should face your fears,' just before she showed her true yaka form and swallowed them up.

'She's helped hundreds of children,' Ianthi went on. 'She knows what's best for troubled kids like you.'

'I'm *not* a troubled kid!' Mythil flared up. He hated her tone. She wasn't a kid taking a kid's side. She was a kid trying very hard to be an adult. And succeeding too, he thought contemptuously. She sounded just like the adults and Mythil was furious at himself for ever having thought she was his friend.

He was so choked up he couldn't say anything else. He wanted to push her roughly away but Archchi had told him that it was cowardly for a boy to hurt a girl. So he turned his back on her and stormed out of the room to find his parents.

He didn't care anymore whether she knew her mother was a yaka or not. She deserved a yaka mother for lying to him and pretending to be his friend, when all the time she was probably spying on him for Aunty Nilmini.

Mythil stalked away into another ante-room filled with old clay pots and cooking utensils in glass cabinets and found that there was no way out of it. He turned to leave and shrank back in horror. There was Aunty Bhishani blocking the doorway.

Trapped!

Wrapping the fall of her grey and white saree around her waist Aunty Bhishani stepped over the threshold and stopped, her eyes gleaming in the lamplight. As she stood there, blocking the doorway something snapped inside Mythil. He flung himself at her, fists flailing, trying to push her away. But she was much stronger than she looked. She grabbed him by his wrists and shook him. Gritting his teeth he tried to pull away from her but she held on tightly.

She was frowning. 'Something has changed,' she said in her sandpapery voice. 'You are not afraid any more. I cannot make you afraid.' Mythil twisted and pulled, struggling to escape her iron grip. She smelt of moth balls.

'I'm *not* afraid of you. Let me go!' Mythil said changing tactics and trying to push her away. But she shook him until he thought his head would fly off.

'Have you lost your gift, boy?' she asked breaking into a deep chesty laugh. 'Your gift of seeing yakas.' She flung him away from her and sent him sprawling across the floor.

Mythil backed up against a display cabinet leaving sweaty palm prints against the glass. 'Yes, I have,' he bluffed. 'I made a deal with a yaka.'

'You didn't,' she said moving towards him. 'You still have that aura around you boy. So you still have the gift. But you have got something more. You have got protection – that's why I can't put fear into you.'

'But I can put fear into you!' Mythil said pulling his pocket-knife out. He fumbled frantically with the blade for a few seconds before managing to unfold the knife. The blade was shimmering blue again.

'Do you think I am scared of a little iron?' she asked, but she didn't come any closer. 'How do you think I exist in your world? Iron hurts, yes, but I have learnt to overcome the pain.' Mythil scrabbled under one of the tall glass display tables and stood up on the other side.

'You don't want to come in contact with this blade,' he said. 'It will electrocute you.'

A curious look came over her eyes. 'Where did you get that knife from? And how do you know so much?'

'I know enough to tell everyone. We'll get a yakadura and he'll send you back.' She came closer and Mythil brandished the knife at her. 'He'll send you back to your world. Where you belong. This isn't your world, is it? What's the matter? Are you scared to go back?'

The yaka narrowed her eyes. 'How do you know so much?' she asked again. She seemed bigger than he remembered. She must be taller than Thaththi, Mythil thought. 'None of your feeble yakaduras can send me back boy. But you have learnt much about us. You have been conversing with our kind, haven't you?' she asked moving closer.

'That could only mean that there actually is a little tree-spirit in that jungle of yours. You weren't imagining it, were you?' Mythil faltered. She knew about Asiri. Aunty Nilmini must have told her.

He backed out of her reach as she moved around the table trying to corner him. It was like playing a deadly game of tag. Although she looked like an old woman, Mythil knew now how strong she was. He was not going to underestimate her strength again. His wrists still stung from where she had gripped them.

'Don't you worry – we'll get him. And you won't escape us for long either my little one.' For a second her eyes glowed – but only for a second. He could see that she was fighting off the effect he had on yakas. She was stopping her face from changing into its yaka form.

'I'm leaving the country,' Mythil said bluffing again. How he wished it was true. He hoped that if they left the country the yakas could no longer touch him.

But Bhishani dashed his hopes. 'Going to Hong Kong perhaps?' she said mockingly. 'So your father got the job?' Mythil could have kicked himself. Thaththi had been speaking to Uncle Anthony about the job, so of course she would know of it. She was a family friend.

'You may be safe from me in Hong Kong but do you think your little jungle is the only place with a portal? There are portals all over the world and the beings that come out of them may be different from us yakas but they won't appreciate your gift any more than we do boy. So you've no escape. They'll destroy you if I don't do it first.'

'You're lying,' Mythil said boldly – far more boldly than he felt. 'You can't kill a human. You're not allowed to. It's the law of the spirits.'

'We have our ways of getting around the law,' she said with a look that nearly froze Mythil's blood. She drew closer. 'But tell me how you got this shield?' she asked leaning over the table and poking at the air around him. 'You still have an aura but it has changed slightly. I can touch you but I cannot put fear in you. Where did you get this protective aura?'

Mythil edged further away from her. She was right, he thought. He was still scared of her but it wasn't the same sort of fear he had had when he first encountered her yaka form on the pavement.

He noticed that his dark blue trousers were dusty from the fall but he didn't dare brush them, fearing that the yaka would make her move. He couldn't understand why she kept saying he had a protective aura. He assumed an aura was some kind of human force field. How was that possible? Was this a trick?

'Have you asked your little tree-spirit for this boon, boy? This protection?'

For a moment Mythil wondered whether Asiri had changed his mind about granting him the second boon.

But Bhishani kept muttering to herself. 'No, no. That can't be right. Where have I seen this type of aura before?'

Mythil felt a slight measure of relief. If Asiri had changed his mind and granted Mythil a second boon the yaka-boy would now be defenceless. He hadn't liked thinking that Asiri had risked his life for him. He didn't want to feel indebted to that irritating little tree spirit. He edged away from Bhishani, closer to the door.

'What is it? What is it?' she went on talking to herself. Her eyes widened suddenly. 'Ah! I have it. You helped him in some way – didn't you? Yes of course. That is it isn't it? You have shown a kindness to him. Not saved a life – that would have made your aura much stronger – but perhaps you spared his life? Yes, that's it.'

Mythil felt the hair rising on the back of his neck. Was she referring to the time when Asiri had been caught in the trap? And he had given him kevili. He remembered now that the tree-spirit had mentioned something about protection.

And then suddenly to Mythil's horror the table was no longer between them. Bhishani walked through it striding towards Mythil. She was almost upon him when he remembered the knife and swiped at her with it. The blunt knife tip just grazed her wrist but it was enough to keep Mythil safe. Blue sparks flashed along the blade and the next moment Bhishani was back on the other side of the table holding her wrist and hissing like an angry cobra.

'That's how you got the tree-spirit in your power, isn't it?' Bhishani rasped, her eyes flashing angrily. 'And the little fool begged you to spare him. That is how you have learnt so much no?'

Bhishani made an impatient noise with her tongue. 'It is of little importance. And as I told you, if I don't get you before you go to Hong Kong, there will be others like me there. Those who have come from other worlds, other portals. Have you never wondered why there are such different stories about different – 'magic' you people call it – magic people? Will you fight them all?' she taunted him.

'But I will tell everyone about *you*,' Mythil said. He felt much bolder now that he knew the effect the knife had on this powerful spirit. 'How you are a yaka. That there are hundreds like you pretending to be human. And I'll find a way to send you back. All of you!'

'Mythil!' His heart leapt. Somewhere in this labyrinthine museum Ammi was looking for him.

'If I don't get to you first, boy,' she said with a dangerous smile. 'You are a very clever little boy to have found out as much as you have. But you're no warrior. You're just a boy. Who will believe you? Even now, your parents think you see yakas because you are worried that they will divorce. Is that not so?'

'That's because of your lies,' Mythil retorted hotly. 'The lies of your friend Nilmini. She's a yaka too, isn't she?'

'Do you think so?' Bhishani asked with a contemptuous smile. 'Do you think she wouldn't have eaten you up when she had you alone in the forest if she was a yaka?'

'Mythie!' Ammi was getting closer. Bhishani had heard her too.

'I'm here, Ammi!' Mythil called out. He smiled grimly at Bhishani. 'She couldn't have done anything to me in the jungle.' Mythil said. 'My family would have known she was a yaka.'

'Ah yes, your family,' she said. 'Troublesome that you have a family. Makes the hunt, shall we say, *interesting* with them around,' she leered at him. 'Oh yes, it is a hunt now my little one and it has begun. We're going to get you and your little yaka friend. It's only a matter of time.' And with that she vanished.

Mythil blinked. He approached the door cautiously but Bhishani had gone.

'There you are Mythil,' Ammi said spotting him peering out of the doorway. 'Come. We're leaving.' Mythil ran over to her and hugged her in relief. 'What was that for?' Ammi asked with slight amusement as she ruffled his hair and held his hand. Mythil cautiously folded the knife and slipped it into his pocket with his other hand. Ammi walked quickly back to the entrance where Thaththi was waiting for them. Mythil looked at his parents. They seemed very angry.

'Oh be reasonable!' Aunty Nilmini was saying to Thaththi in an exasperated tone. 'No harm has come of it!' She looked almost sulky. She doesn't like it when people stop thinking of her as a great psychologist, Mythil thought with some satisfaction.

'We're leaving now Nilmini,' Thaththi said firmly. 'Thank you for trying to help but I think we'll take it from here.'

'Yes, now that you've got the job you no longer need us I suppose,' she retorted rather snappily. She looked very angry indeed and Mythil, who had just dealt with an angry yaka felt glad to have Ammi and Thaththi to protect him. Then Ianthi, Uncle Anthony and Aunty Bhishani came and stood behind Aunty Nilmini. Mythil felt they were outnumbered. He avoided looking at Bhishani.

'That's not the issue, Nilmini,' Ammi said placatingly. 'We appreciate your help. What we're objecting to are your drastic measures regarding our son – we don't think Mythil is ready for a confrontation like this.'

Ammi had on a tight little smile but Mythil knew that smile well. It meant 'I am being nice to you because that is the civilised thing to do but don't push me.' It was Ammi's dangerous smile.

But Thaththi didn't bother with smiles. He had had enough. 'Thank you Anthony,' he said nodding at him in farewell. Uncle Anthony nodded back solemnly. Looking at the opposite group Mythil felt that of the four of them he probably liked Uncle Anthony the most. Then Thaththi and Ammi marched out of the museum with Mythil between them.

When they got into the car, Thaththi started the engine even before closing the door. Aunty Nilmini, Aunty Bhishani and Uncle Anthony stood at the entrance of the museum talking among themselves. Ianthi squeezed in between them and grinned at Mythil. She looked up at her mother and began saying something. Mythil was sure she was telling them that he had said her mother was a yaka too. The car reversed out of the lane and then he was flung back against the seat as Thaththi floored the accelerator.

Mythil's mind was spinning. So many things were whirling round his head. But he knew he was forgetting something important. Something more important than warning Asiri or their lives being in danger. What was it?

Then he remembered what Ianthi had said about his parents getting divorced. His heart sank like a stone. Was it true?

Facing up

It was dark when they reached home. Ammi told Archchi about everything that had happened since they left the house that evening. 'At least it's good news about the job,' Ammi said.

'There's still a lot of uncertainty,' Thaththi said. 'We shouldn't get our hopes up until things are finalised.'

'It'll work out,' Ammi said with a smile.

Archchi smiled too but she didn't look thrilled. 'Let's see if I can rustle up a dinner to suit the occasion,' she said heading for the pantry.

Mythil followed her, leaving his parents to talk about the job. He found Archchi with tears in her eyes in the pantry.

'What's wrong Archchi?' he asked in alarm.

'Oh, I'm just being a silly old woman, Mythie-boy,' Archchi smiled at him.

'Why are you crying?' Mythil asked putting his arm around her waist.

'I was just thinking how much I'll miss you all when you go to Hong Kong, darling,' she said. 'But it will be a good experience for you.' She took out one of her scented handkerchiefs from a pocket in her purple kaftan and wiped her eyes.

'I didn't know we were going to Hong Kong *forever*!' Mythil said.

'You won't send your Thaththi alone!' Archchi exclaimed. She seemed to have pulled herself together. 'He's got a good job and you should all be there to support him as a family. You'll make a lot of new friends and ride on a cable car and swim with the dolphins. It will be lovely!'

'What's a cable car?' Mythil asked.

'There's a magazine on the hall table that Aunty Nilmini brought. It tells you all about Hong Kong with the cable cars and theme parks. You can have a look at it. It's very interesting.'

'Are you sure you're all right Archchi?' Mythil asked.

'Yes, yes. Quite all right darling,' Archchi said with a smile. 'Optimism is my middle name after all.'

'What?' Mythil asked in surprise. He had heard a phrase like that before. Hadn't Serf said something like that? 'What did you say Archchi?'

Archchi laughed. 'You've heard that saying before, no?' she asked going over to the fridge. 'When someone says something is their middle name it means that's what they are like. So when I said optimism is my middle name I was saying that I'm an optimistic person.'

It was like someone had turned the lights on in Mythil's mind. The bahirawaya had said 'Serf is my middle name,' and Mythil had taken it literally. So Serf is not his name at all, Mythil realised clapping a hand to his forehead and feeling embarrassed at his mistake. Just as I got used to calling him that, Mythil thought.

'Don't you want to look at that magazine Mythie?' Archchi asked over her shoulder. 'Learn a little about what Hong Kong is like?'

Hong Kong, he thought gloomily. Mythil drifted into the hall. Will we come back to Sri Lanka to visit Archchi during the holidays like we usually do, he wondered. Would she be able to come and visit them in Hong Kong during term time? His parents had gone to their room. Mythil hoped they wouldn't start another fight. He picked up the magazine and went out on to the veranda.

If what Bhishani said was true, even if he went to Hong Kong he would still see other supernatural beings, he thought sitting under a light and flicking the pages of the glossy magazine. At least with the yakas he knew what to expect. He'd heard about them in folktales and through local TV programmes.

As he leafed through the magazine he watched one of the cats crouching along the floor towards a gecko on the wall. What kind of spirits lived in Hong Kong? Would they want to kill him too? Or would the yakas get to him before that like Bhishani had threatened, Mythil wondered.

The cat leapt at the gecko but missed it. The gecko scurried higher up the wall and out of reach. How long would it be before the yakas took action? Bhishani had said that the hunt had already begun.

A flash of lightning lit up the garden briefly followed a few minutes later by a low rumble of thunder. Mythil wished he could tell somebody about the yakas but he knew Bhishani was right and that no one would believe him. The cat stalked away, twitching its tail angrily.

He pulled out his penknife. It had stopped Bhishani from coming at him. Perhaps he should keep it sharp, he thought. Leaving the magazine on the chair he went back into the pantry. Somehow, as scary as it was to have yakas after him, what depressed him the most was the thought that his parents might be getting divorced. He sighed as he began sharpening the blade against the Emory stone.

'Come and have your dinner Mythie-boy,' Archchi sang out. Mythil could hear the dreaded murmur of his parent's voices. He sighed. They're fighting again, he thought.

'I'm not hungry, Archchi,' he said opening and shutting the knife. Perhaps he should put some engine oil on the hinge so that it would be easier to open, he thought.

'I'll feed you,' Archchi said. 'Just eat what you like,' she pulled up a chair and began mixing the food on his plate. 'I'll give the rest to the cats.' As if it had understood her one of the cats mewed from under the table.

'Where did you find that knife?' Archchi asked him as she fed him a mouthful of string-hoppers and fried fish.

'In the shed,' Mythil replied dully rubbing the knife against the stone. She took a closer look at it as she mixed a little bit of sambol with string-hoppers and a big piece of fish.

'That used to be your Seeya's penknife,' Archchi said serving more kiri hodhi on to his plate. 'I thought I had lost it.'

Mythil looked up at her. Her eyes had gone all misty again. 'Do you want to keep it Archchi?' he asked her.

'No, no,' Archchi said mixing the food into a neat little ball. 'Seeya would have wanted you to have it.' She deftly popped the ball of food into his mouth.

Mythil looked down at the carved handle of the knife as he munched his food. He traced his finger along the dragon carving. So it was his Seeya's knife that he had been using as protection against the yakas. Where had Seeya got such a knife from, he wondered. He broke off a piece of fish and held it out to the cat.

Archchi was ready with the next mouthful. 'Your Seeya was always carving in his spare time. When your Ammi and uncles were little, Seeya used to carve wooden boats and float them down the stream.'

Mythil tossed the piece of fish to the cat who stubbornly refused to come near him. Then he got up and went to the sink. He washed and wiped the pen knife and put it back into his pocket. It seemed a little sharper than before. Anyway, he wasn't in the mood to sharpen it anymore.

'There's another wattakka pudding to finish too. Your Ammi forgot to give it in all that madness at the museum,' Archchi said.

'Madness at the museum,' Mythil smiled wryly. 'Yes, that's what it was.'

He shook his head when Archchi offered him another mouthful of string-hoppers. He couldn't eat anymore even though she tried to coax him.

When did his parents plan on telling him that they were getting divorced, he wondered dejectedly. He'd just have to wait and see. He hated confrontations, so there was nothing else he could do. What if he confronted his parents and they said, yes, Mythil, we're getting divorced tomorrow. Was it better not knowing? If he didn't ask, he wouldn't have to know.

But the uncertainty was upsetting. There were too many things he didn't know. Was there going to be a divorce? Were they going to Hong Kong? Were the yakas going to attack him? He had to find answers for at least some of those questions or he would go mad. He took a deep breath and decided to face Ammi and Thaththi. He had to find out now.

So leaving Archchi in the kitchen he marched along the corridor towards his parents' room. But by the time he got there he was uncertain again. Was this a good idea, he wondered.

He stopped outside their doorway absently locking eyes with the closest yaka mask on the wall. He stuck his lower lip out determinedly. Yes, this was the right thing to do, he told himself.

First, I'll settle this and then I'll deal with you lot, he told the silent masks with more conviction than he felt.

Then he turned and entered the room, pushing aside the curtain with a flourish.

'Thaththi, Ammi, is it true? Are you getting divorced?'

Thaththi and Ammi looked up startled. They were sitting on either side of the big old double bed, Thaththi lounging against the intricately carved bed head and Ammi propped up comfortably on pillows at the other end. A bundle of school test papers and a red pen lay untouched by her side. They didn't seem to have been fighting.

'Who said anything about a divorce?' Thaththi asked, sitting up.

'Ianthi,' Mythil said falteringly.

Thaththi and Ammi immediately exchanged angry looks. 'I knew Nilmini was bad news,' Ammi said reproachfully to Thaththi. 'I'm sure she's not even a trained psychologist – she said she's doing a long distance course, didn't she? That whole thing about seeing yakas in colour or black and white sounded like a lot of hocus pocus to me.'

'She never told me she wasn't qualified,' Thaththi said. 'And to be fair I didn't ask. But even if she had been, all I wanted was an evaluation from her because she's worked with children as a counsellor. I thought that if it was necessary she could recommend a specialist to us after she saw Mythil.'

Ammi turned to Mythil and held her hand out. Mythil ignored it and sat on the edge of the bed.

'Mythil,' Ammi said and then stopped. She seemed to be looking for the right words. 'This hasn't been easy for any of us,' she said. She took a deep breath and continued. 'Being good parents and a good wife or a good husband is not something you are born knowing. And it's not something you learn how to do at school or at campus . . .' she broke off.

'What we are trying to say Mythie-boy,' Thaththi said pulling Mythil up against him, 'is that your Ammi and I have tried very hard to get on together. But it has not always been easy.'

'Especially after Thaththi's magazine closed down,' Ammi put in leaning forward and laying her hand on his knee.

'Yes, and I had to work from home doing freelance work and Ammi had to give tuition and take on any extra work just to make ends meet. It's made us irritable and tired and angry with each other all the time.'

'Don't you love each other anymore?' Mythil asked. Despite all his efforts to control it his voice wavered.

'Of course we still love each other Mythil,' Thaththi said. 'But maybe we're not right for each other. We keep arguing all the time and that's not good for any of us.'

'So you are getting divorced?'

'No sweetheart,' Ammi said. 'We haven't ever discussed divorce. But perhaps we need some time to think about our feelings for each other. That's what we've been talking about all this time. Now that Thaththi has got a new job in Hong Kong he will probably have to leave soon. But your school starts again in two weeks and you can't afford to miss that.'

'Yes, we've been really worried about whether we could keep paying your school fees Mythil. We really didn't want to have to move you to a different school that was more affordable. Getting this job in Hong Kong is a huge relief because it means we can easily afford it. So we thought the best thing would be for you to stay on in school here,' Thaththi said.

'Alone?' Mythil asked feeling tears pricking at his eyelids.

'No I'll be staying with you,' Ammi said. 'And Archchi and your cousins will probably visit us in Colombo more often. You'll be the man of the house. It'll be all right Mythil. Won't it?' Ammi asked sounding anxious. Mythil nodded because he didn't trust himself to speak just then. He had to look down quickly as a tear tumbled down his cheek before he could blink it away.

'And as soon as the term is over we'll fly to Hong Kong to be with Thaththi!' Ammi went on. 'You'll get to go in an aeroplane! You'll like that no?'

Quickly brushing away all traces of the tear from his cheek Mythil turned around so that he could see them both. 'So . . . ?' he began.

'So we thought . . . Ammi and I . . . that we'll take the time apart to look at what our relationship needs,' Thaththi said. 'Maybe things will work out. I've been irritable and bad tempered but now that I have a permanent job I feel much more secure and like my old self again.'

Ammi smiled as Thaththi shook his head and ran his fingers through his hair. 'It's been a nightmare for both of us – trying to find part time work that will keep us going. It's been difficult for all of us.'

Mythil felt guilty at how angry he had been that his parents didn't seem to have time for him. It had never crossed his mind that they were working hard to earn money for them to live and to send him to school. He had thought that parents were like computer game characters. The on-screen fighters could kick or punch or power jump on command. He had always assumed that parents also came pre-programmed to do things parents were supposed to do — like fixing things and looking after kids and making sure there was food on the table. He had never, until that moment, realised how difficult it could be to earn enough money to run a house and family.

Mythil looked at Ammi and Thaththi as if he was seeing them for the first time. They hadn't had it easy either. They didn't have super powers to help them when the odds were against them. They might have been worried and upset all the time but they had kept trying for his sake. Mythil felt his eyes welling up and his chest swelling with pride.

And that's what I have to do with the yakas, Mythil thought. Keep trying and trying until something works out. That's what Serf had said too. Learn to adapt. And because he was still scared of yakas like Bhishani he knew how hard it would be to overcome that fear and find a way to stop her from terrorising him. Adapting wasn't going to be easy but he was determined to try. He took a deep breath.

'So you aren't getting divorced, right?' As he said the words Mythil felt relief flooding through him.

'Not today, or the day after, or the day after that, no,' Thaththi said, putting his arm around Mythil. 'We'll see how this arrangement works. Okay Mythil?'

'Okay,' Mythil said. He would have liked a more positive answer or at least a definite answer but he was glad he had asked the question. At least now he knew what their plans were. He could probably sleep easy tonight.

And then a dazzling flash of lightning and a deafening clap of thunder made them all jump. Almost immediately the lights went off and they were plunged in darkness.

The storm breaks

'Don't move anyone!' Archchi called out from the pantry. 'Wait till I light a lamp.' Mythil edged closer to his father and Thaththi laughed. 'You're not scared of a storm are you, Mythie-boy?'

'Of course he isn't,' Ammi said a little sharply and Mythil hoped they wouldn't start another fight. 'The lightning must have hit a transformer. Goodness only knows when they'll get the electricity back on now.'

A light appeared through the curtain in the doorway. 'Why don't you go and help Archchi light the candles Mythie?' she asked. 'And then you should get to bed. It's almost your bedtime and you've had a long day.'

He certainly had. Mythil slipped off the bed and headed towards the light in the hall. He wasn't afraid of storms. He usually enjoyed watching the lightning slash the sky apart. But tonight, after Bhishani's threats of hunting him down, he just hoped and wished that the storm would blow over quickly. Was it a coincidence that the transformer had been hit by lightning? Or could there be a more sinister reason for the electricity cut? Could the yakas have done it deliberately to warn him that they were around? Mythil shivered as a cold, wet wind blew in from the open windows of the hall.

Seeli was helping Archchi to close the windows. The rain was beating in from the south-west so she shut the windows facing that direction completely. Mythil listened to the big drops of rain splattering against the glass. It was pitch dark outside and he could see nothing. Seeli kept the other windows ajar, 'For some fresh air,' she said. Mythil watched as she made sure the glass panes wouldn't budge in the strong wind by pegging the long brass handles firmly on to the matching brass knobs on the windowsills.

While helping Archchi to light candles around the house he wondered whether there would be time to run into the jungle with an umbrella and warn Asiri that the yakas might be out hunting tonight. That would be the brave thing to do, he thought, even though his heart beat like a piston at the thought of going out into the jungle alone in this storm. But it was too near his bedtime and he knew he would be missed. And probably scolded for getting wet too.

No, that wouldn't do. He'd barely avoided getting into trouble for putting nails in the drains. If Jamis had complained to his parents rather than his grandmother he'd have been in real trouble. He didn't want to be responsible for starting another fight. Besides, he told himself, it wasn't his problem. He had enough problems of his own. The best he could do for Asiri was to warn him early the next morning Mythil decided.

Preparing for bed in his room a little later Mythil watched from his half-open window as the lightning flashed. He caught glimpses of the trees across the stream twisting madly in the wind and rain.

If he had gone through with his plan to warn Asiri that evening the yaka would only have begged Mythil to take him home again, he thought. And with the storm in full sway Mythil would have felt bad to refuse. But how can I bring a yaka into the house, he thought impatiently. Asiri didn't understand humans at all.

A gust of wind made the candle flicker and almost go out. Mythil shut the window completely and wished there were curtains he could draw across the window pane. A feeling of unease crept over him as he thought of the yakas. Could they be in the jungle already?

Even if Aunty Nilmini wasn't a yaka he had seen Bhishani with two other men who could very well be yakas. That meant a minimum of three yakas who might be out hunting at that very moment.

Mythil climbed into bed and lay back on his pillow. He was grateful for the candle Archchi had left in his room, because he could not fall asleep. Thunder crashed outside and lightning lit up his window, illuminating the iron bars through the window pane. Outside he could see trees squirming in the wind, swaying as though possessed.

He shuddered as he remembered what the bahirawaya had said – that the yakas knew that he could see them and that they would do something about it. Bhishani had said the same thing at the museum.

She had also said something that had surprised him. What was it? Ah, yes, she had said his jungle wasn't the only place that had a portal to the yaka world. A portal. That must be like a door, he thought. A secret door. What would it look like? It couldn't be made of wood. It had to be a sort of magic door he guessed.

But where was this portal? He had never seen anything that looked like a magic door. On the other hand he had only explored a very small part of the jungle. Maybe the portal was deep in the heart of it surrounded by impenetrable thorny underbrush. Maybe Bhishani was there already summoning an army of yakas to catch him and Asiri.

Mythil pulled the covers over his face and watched the candle through the thin material. Holding the folded penknife he tried to shut out the questions that came tumbling, helter skelter into his mind.

What kind of plans would the yakas be making? What did they do to people? He remembered seeing exorcist ceremonies in tele-dramas and plays. The people involved seemed to go mad—thrashing and drooling. He groaned to himself. Would the yakas drive him mad? Maybe he should get up and write down everything now while he was still sane.

He lifted a corner of the sheet and looked at the candle. It had almost burnt out. It would not last till he wrote out the entire story, so that wasn't a good idea.

He had to sleep before the candle went out – he thought desperately. Then he would wake up and it would be morning and he would be safe. He tried to think of nothing, but more questions about the yakas welled up in his mind. Then he tried counting sheep like the Muppets did on Sesame Street. He imagined a fence and little cartoon sheep leaping over it. He got to 20 very fast and still felt wide awake. So he slowed down the pace of leaping sheep. The only problem with slowing down was that it gave his mind time to come up with more questions. Then the questions began jostling with the sheep, each trying to jump over that imaginary fence first and his mind got more confused and less sleepy than ever.

When would the yakas attack? Tonight? Tomorrow afternoon? What would they do? Was Asiri okay? How awful he would feel if he went to the jungle tomorrow and Asiri wasn't there! It wasn't that Asiri was his friend, he told himself. He just didn't want to be responsible for the tree-spirit's capture.

The candle spluttered and went out. Mythil drew the covers down to his chin so that he could see the darkened room. He felt he would rather know what to expect than be taken by surprise when the yakas attacked.

Mythil tightened his grip on the sheet and watched the outline of the window for the next flash of lightning. Only the sound of the wind and the rain outside could be heard, punctuated by thunder.

The lightning flashed very briefly and Mythil gasped, the hair rising at the back of his neck. Something was out there. A series of three or four flashes followed in quick succession. Outlined against the window, Mythil saw to his horror a dark silhouette with flowing, wind-blown hair. With a yell that was lost in a clap of thunder Mythil leapt out of bed. Tripping over the covering sheet and almost falling over himself he scrambled toward the doorway. He hit his knee against the wall but his outstretched hands had found the curtain that covered the doorway. Before the next flash of lightning he was outside his room the penknife open and tightly clasped in his hand.

Mythil's knees felt weak. Cold sweat had broken over his brow and upper lip. He wasn't surprised to see blue lights dancing along the knife blade. His guess had been right. The yakas were out hunting for him that night. And they had found their way to his window. His hands were trembling and he had to put the knife down on the cold floor.

Should he run to his parents' room? But what would be the use, he thought despairingly. They would only think it was a bad dream. No, this was something he had to deal with on his own. His breath came out in gasps as though he had been running a marathon. I can do this. I have the knife, he told himself over and over again, hanging desperately to what little courage he could muster.

The blue lights ran along the blade for a whole minute. Then they stopped. Had the yaka left? He crouched at the doorway, holding the curtain steady so that it covered him but also gave him a chink to squint through. The lightning flashed again showing up a silhouette of the iron bars and nothing else. Iron bars. *Iron bars!* Mythil almost wept in relief. The yakas could not get into the house – the window bars were iron.

After midnight

Mythil leaned his forehead against the cold wall and wondered what to do next. He could go back to bed and keep the knife open – if the yakas got near him it would warn him. But what if he fell asleep and didn't see the blue flashes? Or worse, what if he rolled onto the knife and cut himself? He shuddered as he remembered how the knife had slipped so easily into Asiri's arm.

He listened to the 'plink, plink' of rain water falling through a leak in the roof and in to a basin that Seeli had placed somewhere close by. The hall clock struck twelve. It was midnight and a long wait till morning. What should he do?

After two minutes of crouching on the cold floor Mythil decided that he couldn't sleep alone in his bed anymore. The house was still. Everyone must be asleep. If he woke Ammi and Thaththi they would only tell him it was a bad dream and send him back to bed.

Summoning all his courage Mythil stood up. With the penknife held carefully between his teeth, he re-tied his sarong putting a second knot for good measure. Taking the knife in his hand he groped his way towards Archchi's room. The sound of the rain and wind echoed loudly in the corridor. He took deep, gulping breaths to make sure his lungs were full of air so that he could scream loudly at the slightest hint of movement anywhere in the darkened house.

The lightning flashed again and a yaka face seemed to leap out at him from the darkness. He almost screamed but stopped himself in time, clutching at the wall to steady himself. It was only one of the ornamental masks that hung in the corridor. Gathering his wits together, he continued along the corridor averting his eyes from where he knew the masks hung.

At last Mythil found Archchi's room managing not to stumble over the two or three basins and buckets that were collecting rainwater drips from the holes in the roof. Archchi's room windows had wooden shutters which were shut and the sound of the storm was less here. He could hear her 'pfff', 'pfff', breathing and make out where she was lying on the bed. He folded the penknife and nestling it safely in his palm he lay down next to Archchi.

He was too close to the edge of the bed for comfort so he wriggled a little and Archchi woke up with a start. 'Myffil?' she asked and said a few more words he couldn't understand because she was still half-asleep and speaking without her false teeth. She moved to give him more room and put her arm around him. Already he felt much safer.

He thought of Asiri out on this awful night on his own and shivered. Asiri was a spirit who had been around long enough to be able to find shelter from a storm – of that he was quite sure. But if the yakas were after him?

He remembered what Asiri had said about how lucky Mythil was to have the protection of his family. Safe in Archchi's bed, Mythil could fully appreciate this. He knew what it was like to be pitted against the yakas on his own because he had felt very alone in the museum with Bhishani blocking the exit. And that was with his parents being close by. Imagine if he had no parents? No family? No one to run to when danger threatened? He'd be so scared.

And now thanks to him and their conversation at the museum Bhishani had proof that there was a weak yaka hiding in the jungle just waiting to be nabbed. And Asiri had no idea that he had been found out. Mythil tried to tell himself again that it wasn't his problem. But it was no use. He felt guilty for having put Asiri in danger.

Mythil listened to the low, steady rumble of the rain hitting the clay tiles on the roof. Maybe if Asiri was sheltering from the storm he was well hidden and the yakas wouldn't be able to find him. He fervently hoped that was true.

Could he send a thought message to Asiri? Asiri could sense fear – but was it only in the jungle? Mythil closed his eyes and pictured Bhishani as she had been on the pavement outside the shop. How her eyes glowed and how he had been too petrified to move. Then he remembered her in the museum. He remembered the horror of realising just how strong she was despite the fact that she looked like an old woman.

He could feel his heart hammering in his chest – much louder than the sound of the rain. He hoped this was working. Asiri you're in danger he said over and over again. Those were his last thoughts as he fell into a troubled sleep.

Outside the storm howled on. In his dreams the sound changed into the wailing of the yakas – yakas who were chasing him through the jungle. He was flying from tree-top to writhing tree-top, delving in to the earth, hiding behind rocks, swooping up among the threshing branches but still they followed and he couldn't shake them off.

'Where are you hiding little one?' a voice called above the storm and he knew that it was Bhishani. Her minions – two other yakas – split up and swarmed after him threatening to overtake him. They slid easily around slimy, wet tree trunks. They exploded from the earth sending clods of muddy soil flying in their wake.

Fear gripped him making him feel sick. He knew she was coming to gobble him up. That would only make her stronger. He had to escape. But where could he run to? When he thought the yakas had passed him he swooped away from his hiding place inside the hollow of an old tree. But they sensed the movement and doubled back. What should he do now? Where could he go? He was so scared he couldn't think.

I need to hide my fear, Mythil thought in his sleep. I'm making the jungle tremble with it and that will only make it easier for them to find me.

And then the fear overtook him for a moment. How can I *not* fear them, he asked himself. They are after me.

Mythil clenched his fists in his sleep. I must be brave. I am not afraid of them, he said to himself. I have met Bhishani before and she can't scare me anymore.

But they are strong and relentless. How can I escape? There is no one to save me. It is hopeless. I have no power. I am only a weak yaka . . .'

Mythil woke up with a start, beads of sweat standing out on his forehead. *I have no power. I am only a weak yaka.* Those last words, which sounded so familiar now, were still ringing in his ears as he unclenched his fists and opened his eyes to the darkness. He knew what he had just seen. The yakas weren't after him. They were after Asiri. Somehow, he knew this was more than a dream.

And then, for a split second, Mythil was nose to nose with a bug-eyed, frenzied Asiri. 'Please, you have to save me. You're the only one I know . . .' he screamed. And then the room was dark again and only the droning rain and the distant rumble of thunder could be heard.

Mythil's breath came in ragged gasps. He was sure that he had seen Asiri after he had opened his eyes. It wasn't a dream. It was real. And yet, if that were so why hadn't Archchi awoken for the sound of that blood curdling scream? She lay sound asleep beside him.

'You're the only one I know,' Asiri had said, and Mythil knew at once all the things that Asiri hadn't had time to say. He remembered the dread he had felt when he first saw Bhishani's real yaka face when he was out alone with her on the pavement. He had thought he was going to be killed by the yaka and he had wanted so badly to run to his father. To see Archchi and Ammi one more time.

These thoughts had flashed through his mind then and he hadn't even realised it but now faced with Asiri's terror - a terror so familiar to him - he knew what the tree-spirit meant. If Asiri died tonight no one else would know. No one else would miss him. No one would care or shed a tear. And the other yakas knew that.

Something like anger stirred inside him. Anger at the other yakas for preying on the weak and the defenceless. Bhishani and her friends would turn their attention to him after they were done with Asiri. He had to stand up to them sometime and this was as good a time as any. Perhaps together he and Asiri stood a better chance. And he had the knife. Asiri had nothing. And the yakas thought he was alone. He would prove them wrong.

We're not friends, Mythil thought, carefully moving Archchi's arm off him and slipping out of bed. But no one deserves to die like that. No one deserves to be bullied and frightened just because they are small or weak. It isn't fair, Mythil thought, groping his way towards his room. It is time to stop them. It is time to stand up and fight. 'Fight, fight, *fight!* Mythil said in a fierce whisper, punching the air each time he said the word. That action gave him courage.

He unfolded his penknife outside his room door. No blue lights danced along its blade. The yakas were gone from the garden. They were in the jungle, just as he had seen in his dream. Asiri didn't have much time, he thought. He marched into his room boldly. Quickly changing into his shorts and putting on his slippers Mythil pocketed the knife and left the room.

He padded noiselessly to the side door and fumbled with the locks. At last the door was open and he was out in the veranda. The rain had lessened now but the thunder still rumbled. It was much lighter outdoors than in the house and much cooler. Cold rain drops stung his face and body as he stepped outside and a chill wind made him shiver.

Should he take the nails in addition to his knife, he wondered as he sprinted to the upturned pot. A flash of lightning lit up the garden and in that instant he saw that his hiding place had been discovered. The flowerpot had been overturned, the nails scattered and the ornament taken.

Jamis! Mythil thought angrily. The gardener must have found his hiding place and the ornament. Tomorrow he'd get into trouble for robbing the ornament. But he didn't have time to think about that now. He had to face the yakas. And he had to stop them from getting to Asiri.

Taking a deep breath he ran towards the jungle.

The portal opens

By the time Mythil got to the stream his clothes were dripping wet. The stream was twice its size and almost swept him off his feet as he tried to cross it. But eventually he waded across and was in the jungle.

Now how could he find Asiri? He closed his eyes to see whether he could sense the jungle tremble. All he could feel was the thudding of his own heart.

The clearing, he thought. The bahirawaya's clearing was probably the best place to start. He had been there so many times now that he was sure he knew how to get there even in the darkness of the jungle. He started running.

There was no point in being cautious. The entire jungle seemed to be in motion. The wind howled through the trees, shaking every leaf and twig. He would not be able to make out a pouncing yaka in all that commotion and hoped they were too preoccupied with their chase to notice him. He was almost at the clearing when he thought he heard a scream and then suddenly a bright light shone out from among the trees.

Mythil raced towards it. Through the trees he could see that the light was shining on the giant banyan tree – the tree that stood on the bahirawaya's rock. He scrambled through the spiky, wet undergrowth his feet slipping on his muddy slippers. Hiding behind a tree he pulled out the knife and peered out to see what was happening.

In the clearing three towering figures floated above the cowering shape of Asiri. One of them had flowing hair and in her palm was something that radiated a bright green light. Shielding his eyes Mythil squinted at it and gasped – it was his ornament. The one he had stolen from the shop.

'Won't you agree to be my slave little one?' Bhishani's hoarse voice rasped out over the sound of the rain. 'Really, it's not so bad. Or would you rather go back to our world? You know how it works. If you give yourself to me willingly we could both be far more powerful. Aren't you sick of being a weakling? Wouldn't you like to taste power for a change?'

In his yaka form Asiri crouched down as though trying to melt into the rock and Mythil thought he could hear him moaning. How small he looked compared to the awesome figures of the other yakas. Though her back was to him Mythil could see that Bhishani's skin was green and her body was covered in powerful sinewy muscles. Tattered strips of cloth covered parts of her body, thrashing about like her streaming wind-blown hair. He could see powerful muscles ripple under the hairy bodies of the other two yakas as well. They were hooting with laughter. Poor Asiri was no match for them.

But their taunts made Mythil angry. They were like bullies in the school playground who always picked on the smaller, weaker kids when they were on their own. He knew how wretched it felt to be at the mercy of powers that were greater than him and he couldn't stand it.

With a roar he dashed across the clearing and then everything went into slow motion. Bhishani was the first to turn her head and Mythil noticed her eyes bulge in shock as he launched himself at her. His left hand reached out for the ornament as Bhishani swung around to face him with a snarl.

One of the others, a yaka with boar-like tusks, turned and lunged out at him missing by inches. Like a well aimed torpedo Mythil was heading directly for Bhishani. She started to move her hand out of his reach but it was too late. Mythil's fingers closed around the ornament just as Bhishani grabbed his shoulder with her other hand and flung him against the rock.

Mythil had the breath knocked out of him as he slid down next to Asiri. Gasping for air he held the ornament in front of him in his closed fist. The green light streamed out through his fingers and he thought he saw a look of horror cross Bhishani's face. He brought his other hand up to brandish the knife but it came up empty. He had lost the knife.

'Don't come closer,' he gasped trying to catch his breath as the yakas closed in on him. 'I'll break it.' Mythil felt Asiri draw closer to him. He was no longer moaning.

'Stop!' Bhishani screamed at the other two yakas. Her order arrested them in mid flight. One of them ground his fist in his palm as if he was holding himself back with difficulty.

Even though her face wasn't human Mythil could make out the crazy rage that ran through Bhishani's fearsome features. She raised her hand as though to strike him. Then she seemed to master her emotions. Her laugh boomed out above the noise of the storm.

'How nice of you to join us, boy! We were wondering how to draw you out of that house away from the protection of your family. It's so kind of you to oblige us like this. Now we can finish this business tonight.'

'I'll break it,' Mythil said again his breath coming in choking gulps.

'Oh I don't think so,' Bhishani said. She closed her fingers and Mythil felt his t-shirt being gripped at the neck. He panicked. She wasn't even touching him and yet he was being lifted off the ground and drawn towards her! He was petrified by the three yakas floating in front of him. Their eyes glowed red and their fangs gleamed in the light of the ornament that he clutched so tightly in his hand.

Then suddenly when he was just a foot away from them Asiri leapt up from his crouching position with a cry and flung his arms around Mythil's neck and waist pulling him back down towards the foot of the rock. Mythil hung on to Asiri with one arm and brought his other arm down against the rock behind them smashing the ornament.

'You fool!' Bhishani howled.

The darkness was blinding. 'Run!' Mythil told Asiri urgently. 'Run, before they realise what's happening!' He was still in Bhishani's invisible grip and couldn't move.

'I'm staying,' Asiri said still hanging on grimly to him and Mythil could feel him change back into his boy form. Then both of them were lifted off the ground and roughly pulled apart by the yakas on either side of Bhishani.

'You little fools!' Bhishani screeched. 'Do you think you can escape me?' Her awful face was just inches from his and Mythil was so terrified that he hardly had time to wonder how he was able to see her in the dark. And then it wasn't so dark anymore. A strange blue light was filling the clearing. Bhishani turned away from Mythil, her nostrils flaring. He strained to look over his shoulder and see what was happening.

A roaring blue vortex had opened up in the rock where he had smashed the ornament. Flashes of light dazzled them and enormous dark shadows loomed within its yawning depths.

'Now look what you've done. You've opened the portal,' Bhishani bellowed. Her eyes gleamed even brighter. She moved her face to within inches of Mythil again. This time her voice was silky smooth.

'There's only one way to close it you know. Do you know how? The only way to close it is to feed it a sacrifice.' Her green skin and glowing eyes made her a terrifying spectre. She took a deep breath and bellowed, 'Throw them in!'

The boys screamed and struggled as the yakas swooped down towards the vortex with them. 'Wait!' Bhishani said and the yakas paused. 'There's no rush. Let's do this nice and slowly.'

The yaka who held Asiri captive gave a nasty laugh. Then both yakas swooped closer to the opening and pushed the boys' faces towards the swirling blue chaos.

'That's where you're going my little ones,' Bhishani screeched. 'And there's no returning . . . ever! This is the night you give up your miserable little lives. How does it feel?'

Held in front of the vortex Mythil felt sick with fear. It felt like he was being drawn out of his body and into the swirling chaos in front of him. He felt too weak to struggle anymore. I'm going to die, he thought. I'm going to die and no one knows.

The secret of the ring

'How do you feel now little ones?' Bhishani taunted from behind them. 'Are you ready to say good bye?'

'Oh but surely you're not taking your leave so soon?' a cheery voice suddenly piped up startling everyone. Without letting go of their captives the yakas drew back from the vortex hissing like snakes. Leaning casually against the rock next to the portal, almost invisible against the glare of it, stood the bahirawaya.

Serf! Mythil almost cried with relief. He didn't know why he felt so happy to see him. There was no guarantee that the man would be on their side. But the contrast between the fearsome yakas and the smiling bahirawaya was so great that Mythil's heart filled with hope.

'You!' Bhishani said and Mythil saw her eyes bulge with fear.

'How do you do?' Serf said with a slight bow. Then as though a thought had just crossed his mind he turned to Mythil and murmured from the corner of his mouth. 'Er . . . how do you do means hello.' He turned back to Bhishani.

'Yes, we meet again,' the bahirawaya beamed at Bhishani, his silver chain and bracelets gleaming in the eerie blue light. Mythil noticed that his long hair was piled up on top of his head this time and kept in place by a silver crown. The bahirawaya seemed much more official-looking somehow than when Mythil had met him earlier. Instead of a loin cloth he wore what looked like a sarong made of peacock feathers. Despite being so much smaller than the yakas in stature Mythil thought the bahirawa lord cut a far more impressive figure.

'You have no power,' Bhishani said hoarsely.

'Not while you had my ring,' Serf said. 'But as you can see it is now in my hand.' Mythil squinted against the light and realised that the vortex was rimmed by a huge silver hoop. The bahirawaya had his hand on its rim. Is that what Bhishani had stolen from him, Mythil wondered, a ring?

And then he remembered. The green, glass trinket had made a tinkling noise when he shook it. He had thought it was broken, but perhaps that was the sound of the ring inside it. And now somehow it had magically expanded to become a portal. He was so taken up with solving this mystery that he almost missed the next bit of conversation.

'And the one who opened the portal can choose to grant me, or you, the rights to the ring,' the bahirawaya was saying. 'Whom do you think he will choose?'

Bhishani turned towards Mythil, her eyes burning and her hand reaching out for him. 'If I kill him first . . .' she hissed.

'Say you choose him, say you choose him!' Asiri cried out and ended in a horrible choking sound as his captor grabbed him around the neck.

'I do! I choose you!' Mythil blurted out finding his voice at last as he felt the vice-like grip around his neck tightening. 'I choose Serf. I mean, I mean, Lord Bahirawa.'

'Serf?' the bahirawaya looked amused. 'Well that *is* my middle name after all,' he said winking at Mythil. 'It'll do nicely.' Then his voice turned business-like. 'And now, first things first.'

He snapped his fingers at the yakas holding the two boys. Mythil and Asiri were dropped from a height of three feet or so as the two yakas released them with a howl, their hands covering their faces. Mythil landed on the muddy ground with a thump and something hard fell on him.

'Ow!' he said rubbing his head. And then he almost jumped out of his skin as he saw what looked like the faces of their captors on the ground. He realised that the spirits themselves had turned into pale blue ghosts. The only substantial thing about them seemed to have been their masks. The vortex roared louder and like smoke in an exhaust fan the two howling spirits were pulled into the portal. Mythil looked across at Asiri who was staring bug eyed at the vortex and the bahirawa lord.

'You're not going to do that to me,' Bhishani said fiercely.

'The last time we met you had your minions and your master plan,' Serf said with a steely smile and Mythil realised with a shiver that for all his cheerfulness Serf was not someone you'd want to cross.

'You don't have any of them now. If you're going to run be my guest, but remember the rules. When the portal is open you cannot leave without my permission.' The bahirawa lord crossed his arms and the silver bracelets glistened as if they were on fire – a blue fire.

'I'm more powerful than you think,' Bhishani spat at him. She swooped away from him until she was about ten feet up in the air, glaring down at them with her glowing eyes.

'Why? Because you've enslaved so many lesser yakas?' Serf asked in a voice that was as hard as steel. 'Didn't it ever cross your mind that you'd have to pay for what you've done at some point?'

'Try and make me!' Bhishani screamed ripping a hole in the canopy of banyan tree leaves as she soared up into the sky.

'Ai-aiyo,' the bahirawaya sighed shaking his head. 'She never tires of 'testing' her limits.' Then he looked at the boys with a twinkle in his eye. 'I'm sorry. "Testing her limits", do you know what that means?' Asiri and Mythil nodded wordlessly.

'Of course you do,' Serf said, seeming to hide a smile. He didn't seem to be in the least bit worried that Bhishani was escaping.

'Would you mind if I borrowed this for a minute?' the bahirawaya asked holding something out to Mythil. It was his penknife. Mythil shook his head numbly, not trusting himself to speak just yet.

'Thank you,' Serf said, 'And in return for your kindness let me show you some magic.' His eyes gleamed as he whispered something to the knife and like a skyrocket it soared after Bhishani leaving a blue and silver trail behind it.

He stood looking up at the sky almost like a child waiting for a fire cracker to explode. Asiri edged closer to Mythil and they both peered up through the leaves of the banyan tree.

Then there was a flash of light. That seemed to have been the cue he was waiting for. Serf began pulling on the silvery blue trail left by the knife as though hauling down a kite in a hurry. Looking back up through the leaves Mythil noticed a large dark shape hurtling down towards them. He and Asiri cowered instinctively expecting Bhishani to come crashing down on them through the branches.

'Don't worry you two. You have nothing to fear from her anymore,' Serf called out to them. He stopped hauling on the shiny ribbon and snapped his fingers. The dark shape had just hit the top branches when it disappeared and a few seconds later Bhishani's 'face' landed with a thump on the ground along with Mythil's penknife. The rest of her broke into several streaming blue wisps.

'I will have my revenge!' one of the wisps said as it was sucked into the portal.

'I don't think so,' the bahirawaya told the rumbling, roaring vortex – for nothing more was left of the spirit that was Bhishani. 'You just ceased to exist here.'

He tapped the rock and with that the portal began to close, the silver hoop growing smaller and smaller until it was the size of a normal ring. The vortex still raged within its centre emitting enough light for them to see each other by. The other blue wisps whizzed away into the night sky. The bahirawaya didn't seem to be worried by that either.

Mythil and Asiri exchanged glances. Were they safe? Was the adventure over? Now what was going to happen?

Bhishani's story

'Let's not close the portal just yet. We need a bit of light and peace and quiet to finish this business,' Serf said with a grin at the two boys. 'While the portal is open we are surrounded by a force field that will keep those spirits in and any other disturbances out. It's useful magic, isn't it? Keeps the rain out too.'

Mythil thought that the bahirawaya sounded very glad to have his powers back. But so much had happened since he stepped out of the house into the storm that he was still a bit dazed by it all.

Asiri too just stared open-mouthed, hanging on to his face with both hands as though he thought it might pop off. Mythil guessed that he was wondering whether he was safe or whether this strange being's job was to send all spirits like him back through the portal.

He squinted up at the luminous blue wisps of fast-moving smoke that were still whizzing around above the branches of the banyan tree. They seemed to be trying to escape. Perhaps they hadn't realised yet that the force field held them trapped within the bahirawaya's power.

There were so many questions buzzing around in Mythil's head that he didn't know where to start. He opened his mouth to ask a question but the bahirawaya spoke first.

'Let's get comfortable first, shall we?' Serf asked. 'Explanations are going to take a while I can tell you.' He cracked his knuckles, looking very pleased with himself.

Mythil gasped at what happened next although Asiri didn't seem too surprised. Several overhanging roots from the banyan tree poured down around them like wax forming three comfortable swing like seats for them to sit on. Another creeper with small fragrant flowers and leaves wove itself in among the thicker banyan roots forming a soft, cushion for them to sit on.

'Up you get,' Serf told Asiri and Mythil. Asiri was the first to try it. He was already swinging in his hammock grinning delightedly when Mythil got gingerly on to his. The hammocks formed a tight circle underneath the banyan tree and within that circle no rain fell and no cold wind blew. In fact it was quite warm and Mythil thought distractedly that he would soon be dry.

Serf sat cross-legged on his hammock. 'Just one last thing before we start our story,' he said taking off one of his bracelets. Both boys watched in silence as he placed it on his palm and tapped it with a pudgy finger. Then he picked it up and it was stiff like a bangle.

Serf held the bangle up in the air and started muttering a low chant. One of the blue wisps detached itself from the others, floated down through the branches and disappeared into the silver hoop.

'What . . . what are you doing to it?' Asiri stammered. He clamped a hand over his mouth as soon as he spoke. With his other hand he was clutching on to his seat as if afraid that he too might be drawn into the alluring silver circle.

'I'll explain in a little while,' Serf said shortly. He kept on muttering and one by one the spirits floated down, zoomed in through the silver hoop and disappeared.

Were they trapped inside the bracelet? Mythil wondered. His eyes rested on the masks on the muddy ground and then on the still open penknife. Its blade glinted blue. He slipped off his hammock and picked up the knife. The last of the blue spirits had disappeared into Serf's silver hoop now.

'This . . . this knife,' Mythil stammered at last. 'It was my grandfather's.'

Serf nodded placing the silver hoop on his palm once more. 'Your grandfather was a brave and sapient warrior, young Mythil . . .'

'Serpent?' Asiri blurted out before he could stop himself.

'*Serpent* warrior?' Mythil asked in horror at the same time.

'No, no, *sapient*! Wise.' Serf said earnestly. 'I really must try harder,' he muttered to himself in an exasperated tone. 'I'm such an anachronism.' Then he continued. 'Your grandfather helped to police the spirit world and send back renegade spirits, like the one you just helped me with.'

'So...so you only send back bad spirits, lord bahirawa.' Asiri stammered.

'And you don't send humans through the portal?' Mythil asked folding the knife and tucking it into his pocket. 'So, it's not true that human sacrifices were made to you?'

'First of all let's stop with the lord business, shall we? A new era calls for a new name. And Serf will do fine,' he chuckled and this time Mythil smiled too.

'I feel like I've been trapped in a time lock and only just been released. I need a make-over. And secondly,' he threw back his head and laughed. It was a deep, mellow laugh that was infectious. Mythil and Asiri exchanged glances and found themselves relaxing and grinning.

'Secondly, the story about human sacrifices was something we started to keep people away from the portals,' Serf said. 'And a few of our brave human friends would step through a portal for effect when other humans were watching just to 'prove' it was true. It was a great way of keeping people away.'

'Could they come back?' Mythil asked. 'I mean the people who went through it.' He didn't think he would ever be brave enough to step through the portal. The feeling of being near it had been too sickening.

'Oh yes, easily,' the bahirawaya said. 'As long as one of my kind was at hand to bring them back.'

'And my grandfather?' Mythil asked, 'Did he go through the portal too? Did he really die of a heart attack like my Archchi says or did the spirits get him?'

'You certainly have a vivid imagination, Mythil. Er...imagination? Oh yes, of course you know what that means,' Serf said hurriedly swallowing a smile as Mythil started to look cross. 'But every story has a beginning,' he said, 'So why don't we start there?' The boys nodded and Mythil got back on to his hammock.

'Well, to go back to the very beginning, a long, long time ago, it was discovered that it is possible for beings to travel from one world to another,' Serf said and then stopped. 'But can you understand the concept of different worlds?'

'Yes, I do,' Mythil said, leaning forward, eager to learn more. 'There are so many TV programmes and movies about rifts to different worlds. It's easy to understand.' Then it was his turn to hesitate. Would Serf know what a TV was?

'Er ... a TV programme is a modern way of telling a story,' Mythil said, wondering how to explain what a television was to someone who had lived in the jungle for who knew how long. 'It's a sort of box which has different um ... story tellers.'

'Ah, yes, there's a little house at the edge of the jungle on the other side and the old man and his wife there watch this TV box quite a lot. I suppose they aren't interested in watching the programmes that talk about other worlds.' Serf said, 'So I must have missed them.'

He stopped as he saw the surprised looks he was getting from the boys. 'Well, the TV faces the window you see and I get a bird's eye view of it from the branch of a jak tree outside. I always watch the tele-dramas with them. I suppose I'll have to give that up now that I have my real job back again!' He sighed as though this was a big drawback.

Mythil laughed out loud at the idea of Serf watching tele-dramas from a jak tree but Asiri spoke up, 'I never knew there was another house near the jungle,' he said. 'And I thought I knew this place so well.'

'It's not your fault you couldn't find it young Asiri,' Serf chuckled. 'I use that house to keep up to date with what's going on in this world so a long time ago I made sure it was hidden from spirits.'

'Is Archchi's house protected like that too?' Mythil asked.

'The house is protected, yes. No dangerous spirit can enter it. But the garden isn't. You found that out tonight didn't you?' Serf asked. He was pulling out another one of his many bracelets now. 'You hid the ornament with the ring in the garden and Bhishani was able to get at it.'

'And I thought that was Jamis,' Mythil said. He was quiet for a minute as he thought things out.

'So does that mean that Aunty Nilmini isn't a yaka? Because she was able to enter the house without any problem.' He felt a little disappointed. 'I sort of thought she was a yaka,' he said in a small voice.

'Nilmini is no yaka,' Serf said. He had been tapping the second bracelet too but stopped now turning quite serious. 'But she had a little sister who had the gift of seeing spirits. No one believed her of course – not even Nilmini. Then the spirits found out about her. It was Bhishani who tricked the little girl into fording a river which was too deep and she drowned.'

Mythil felt horrified. That's what'll happen to me if any other yaka gets their hands on me, he thought fearfully, beads of sweat forming on his brow. They'll trick me into doing something that'll get me killed.

Serf was continuing with his story, 'Ever since the day her little sister died Nilmini made it her mission to help troubled children. She thought her sister was troubled and seeing things. Things that didn't exist. She took a special interest in you ...'

'Because I said I was seeing yakas like her sister,' Mythil finished.

'Quite right. She had no idea that the woman who befriended her and helped her in her shop was the very monster who was responsible for the death of her sister,' Serf said.

His eyes had gone all cold and ferocious and the flowers around him withered. 'Bhishani stuck to Nilmini like sticky koholla because she knew that the ability to see spirits runs in the family. So she made herself indispensable.'

'That's why Ianthi took her side,' Mythil exclaimed, forgetting his own fears for a minute. 'Bhishani must have been particularly nice and friendly to her so that she'd know if Ianthi ever developed the power to see yakas.'

'Yes, you're probably right,' Serf said and the flowers around him began springing to life again one by one. The second silver hoop in his hand kept growing as he spoke. 'Bhishani was one of the most artful spirits I ever encountered. Ianthi probably loves her like a grandmother. They will certainly be very sad when Bhishani never returns home.'

Mythil hadn't thought of that. He picked one of the fragrant flowers off the hammock and sent it twirling down to the jungle floor below. If Ianthi loved Bhishani as much as he loved Archchi she would certainly be very upset. He knew he would be desperately sad if Archchi suddenly disappeared.

Perhaps he had been too hasty in judging Ianthi, Mythil thought. After all if he looked at the whole thing from Ianthi's point of view her actions made sense. Her mother had told her Mythil was a troubled kid so she had thought she was helping when she made friends with Mythil. But when Mythil had accused her mother of being a yaka – he felt very embarrassed as he thought about that now – she had obviously thought he was mad.

Maybe someday I'll be able to explain things to her, he thought. Then he turned his attention back to the bahirawaya.

The secret revealed

'Now where were we before we began talking about Bhishani?' Serf asked. The silver hoop in his hand was now about the size of a basketball ring and he tapped it once more to stop it from expanding any further. 'Oh yes – I was saying there are many worlds and you were saying you understood. How far we have digressed!'

Mythil and Asiri exchanged glances. 'Digressed?' Asiri mouthed at Mythil and Mythil bit his lip to keep from giggling. It really was funny how Serf couldn't seem to stop using big words even though he was trying so hard not to.

'Right, now as I was saying we discovered that there were portals between worlds,' the bahirawaya said. 'So some of us formed a league, er . . . um a team? Ah yes, you know what league means – the league of gatekeepers I suppose you could call us.'

The league of gatekeepers, Mythil thought. That sounded intriguing.

'We had to form a league,' the bahirawa lord continued. 'If people could travel through worlds in armies imagine the havoc they could wreak! And that wasn't all. Such mass-scale movements would make the portals unstable.

'With us in charge no one went in or out without our permission. It wasn't a foolproof system but we did the best we could. The people of Bhishani's world, that was your world too Asiri,' he said looking kindly at Asiri. 'They were in danger of being destroyed – I'm not sure what the circumstances were – but they discovered a rift through which they could escape their world. When one world is in danger of destruction we allow bands of people from that world into a different world.

'The people can only enter and stay in these other worlds as spirits,' Serf said as he pushed his hand in through the large silver hoop. Instead of appearing on the other side his hand simply disappeared inside the hoop.

This time Mythil was less surprised. He was beginning to understand that the bracelets were also part of some sort of holding case or bag that they couldn't see. Serf was keeping the rescued spirits in the first bracelet bag. And now he was scrabbling about inside the second invisible bag for something else.

'We hoped that some day they would be able to return and their way of life would be preserved,' Serf went on, taking his hand out of the ring for a moment to straighten his silver crown which was beginning to tilt.

'While they are out of their own world we make sure that the memories of their world are locked away inside their heads so that it can be preserved unspoilt until they can return to the world they were born in.'

That's why Asiri keeps saying things are written in his head, Mythil thought as he watched Asiri rub his head distractedly. And why he couldn't remember anything about the world he came from.

'You mean their memories are written in the masks?' Mythil asked pointing at Bhishani's mask on the ground.

'Yes,' Serf said. 'Without the masks their spirit forms couldn't survive outside their own world. It's the masks that keep each spirit intact.' Then his eyes lit up and he said, almost to himself, 'Ah yes, this will do.'

With that he pulled out a mask from within the rim of the bracelet. The boys gasped in surprise.

'What do you think?' Serf asked the boys. The mask Serf had pulled out didn't look as fancy as the ones that hung in Archchi's house. But he seemed to be very proud of it. 'It was made by the bahirawa lords a long time ago. The gate keepers of each world are responsible for making the masks for the spirits.'

'Are there bahirawa lords in every world?' Mythil wondered out loud. This mask was mostly blue and black with bulgy eyes and teeth.

'No, not in every world,' Serf said. 'There's an assortment of different beings for different portal zones and different worlds. This particular portal zone is run by the bahirawa lords. So every gatekeeper you will find in this area will be a bahirawa lord.' Laying aside the large hoop he took the smaller one and pulled out a wriggling blue wisp as though it was a fluffy scarf.

Holding the mask in the other hand he pulled the blue smoky spirit into the back of the mask. A bright blue light flashed out across the clearing. Mythil's eyes watered at the sudden brightness but he was eager to see what happened next so he didn't look away. In an instant there stood before them a small yaka – a little smaller than Asiri. It staggered bewildered and disoriented but before it could even look around Serf tapped it and said, 'Be gone,' and it disappeared.

'Remember I said that a yaka's memories of their home world are written in their masks?' the bahirawaya asked. 'Well when a mask is taken off a yaka he or she gets back those memories and the mask itself turns into a simple wooden one like the one you see on the ground,' he said pointing to Bhishani's mask. 'As soon as spirit and mask are one again our little yaka's memories get transferred to the mask. And the mask becomes more than just a piece of decorated wood.

'Anyway that's how the people of your world entered this world Asiri,' Serf continued. 'But when they got here some of them found ways of enslaving their own kind and of terrorising the people of this world. As gatekeepers we could not intervene. Our power centred on the portals.'

Mythil began to feel sober again. He had been hoping that their new friend would be powerful enough to protect him from the yakas. This didn't sound promising.

'We depended on people like your grandfather to help protect the weaker spirits,' Serf said. 'Like you, your Seeya had the power to see yakas.'

'Who gave him that power?' Mythil asked looking suspiciously at Asiri.

'Not me!' Asiri said, almost falling off his hammock trying to defend himself. 'I told you! I was somebody's slave already. I wasn't around here.'

'Mythil, your grandfather already had the power to see spirits,' Serf said gently. 'He was born with it but kept it secret from everyone. As you have found out it's not easy to get other people to believe you have this gift.' The bahirawaya glanced at Mythil to see how he was taking this news. Noting that the boy was listening attentively he continued.

'Unlike your talent though, your Seeya's power allowed him to see a dim aura around a spirit so he could tell a human from a yaka without them knowing. It was easier for him to keep his secret. Your gift is much more powerful. It forces spirits to reveal themselves against their will.'

'That's what I told you,' Asiri said triumphantly.

'Well it's nothing to be happy about,' Mythil said shortly. He couldn't keep the sharpness out of his voice. 'Like I told *you* it only makes me an easy target for the yakas. And it's all thanks to your boon Asiri.'

'No it's not Mythil,' Serf said surprisingly. 'You were born with this gift.'

Mythil and Asiri stared at him open-mouthed. Then Mythil found his voice. 'That can't be true. I never saw any yakas until I met Asiri. And he said he put a spell on me.'

'It's true Lord . . . er Serf,' Asiri said in a small voice. 'I was lonely and I wanted a friend so I gave Mythil a boon that would allow him to see me. I thought we could be friends. I never meant for this to happen – for him to become a target for the other spirits and all . . .'

'Hold on Asiri,' Serf said with an amused smile, 'It takes a lot of power to give a boon like that. A boon that would allow a human to see every yaka. Do you think you could have done that?' Both boys looked confused. What was Serf saying?

'Mythil was born with the gift of seeing spirits. Wait a bit, until I tell you the whole story.' Serf said before they could interrupt him again. 'No one can tell why some, very few, people can see spirits while so many others can't. As I said earlier it usually runs in the family. Your seeya worked in partnership with a spirit who called himself Dhiyes. After your seeya died, whenever a baby was born into his family Dhiyes would visit the house across the stream to see whether the child had the gift and needed protection.'

'But the house is protected isn't it?' Mythil interrupted. 'How could he get in?'

'The house is protected from unknown spirits or those that would bring harm to the people inside,' the bahirawaya explained patiently. 'Dhiyes was a friend of your grandparents so he could enter without a problem.

'He visited when you were still a baby Mythil. You took one look at him and he was forced to show his real yaka face. Of course no one else could see this but he was quite shocked by how powerful your gift was. He realised at once how this would make you a target for other power-hungry yakas.

'I was locked out of my portal by that time so I was powerless to help him. He did the only thing he could. He granted you a boon that blocked you from using this power. But it took a lot of his own power to do this and so now he is in hiding and it will be many centuries before he can begin defending weak spirits again.'

Mythil felt his head spinning from all this information. So he wasn't going mad. He had been born with the power to see the spirit world. But until Asiri accidentally broke the mind blocks that had been placed on him as a baby he hadn't had any clue about his special 'gift'. He started to run his fingers through his hair and quickly stopped realising that they were caked with dry mud from his adventures that night.

'Why do yakas like Bhishani want to destroy people like me, Serf? People who can see them?' Mythil asked.

'Their first choice is not to destroy people like you,' Serf said pulling out another mask. 'They need you to point out to them who is a yaka and who isn't. Because, as Asiri could tell you, if a yaka is in human form and manages to hold on to that disguise other yakas can't tell that they're spirits. Even with Nilmini's younger sister, Bhishani first tried to use her to find other yakas. But as young as she was the child refused. She threatened to tell her parents about Bhishani . . .'

'I did too,' Mythil said remembering his encounter with Bhishani at the museum. 'So that's why she said she would get rid of me.'

'Was a spirit responsible for Mythil's grandfather's death?' Asiri asked in the silence that followed.

'Yeah, I'd like to know that too,' Mythil said quietly. 'I guess yakas like Bhishani would make it their mission to get rid of people like Seeya and me who wouldn't help them.'

'That's true, but no,' Serf said firmly. 'Your Seeya died of a heart attack. The yaka I told you about - Dhiyes - the one who used to work with your grandfather in policing the other yakas, he was with your Seeya when he died, Mythil. There was no foul play. None of the other spirits knew about your grandfather's talent. Those who did were those we sent through the portal.'

'Until Bhishani stole the ring from you?' Mythil asked.

'Yes,' Serf sighed pushing his crown back in place again. He fused another blue wisp with a mask and made the yaka that appeared vanish again. 'She and other power-hungry, renegade spirits like her were going around either trapping the bahirawayas on this side, like they did to me, or sending them through the portal and destroying the ring that opened it.'

They all looked at the ring on the rock and the swirling blue vortex within its small circumference.

'So portals across the land were being closed down. I knew this and I was on my guard but on that occasion Bhishani was too clever for me. Luckily for her she picked a night when your seeya and the family had gone away on a trip. Not even Dhiyes was around. Bhishani got one of her minions to take on the form of a bahirawaya.

'Now as I said earlier we bahirawayas cannot go far from a portal. If we do we become weaker than new born human babies. The yakas had found out about this . . .' Here his eyes became cold and fierce again.

'No doubt they'd found this out when they tortured the bahirawayas that were trapped at this end of a portal. So one of the yakas transformed himself into a dying bahirawaya and came shrieking towards me that night. Bahirawayas live for much, much longer than humans so it's rare to see one dying. This one looked like he was in such pain – such agonised screaming . . .' Serf ran a hand across his face as if trying to ward off the memory. Mythil and Asiri were riveted by the story.

'And then what happened?' Asiri mouthed.

'I knew the only way to save him was to get him through the portal fast. And that's what those yakas were hoping for. As soon as I had the portal open they swarmed in on me and tried to force me through it. They'd found a way to break through the portal's force field. But because I had been expecting an attack like that I was able to escape.'

'How?' Asiri asked leaning forward in his hammock.

'I had created a wormhole, a sort of mini portal of my own which took me to that house I mentioned earlier.'

'Where you watch TV?' Asiri asked.

Serf smiled. 'Yes, and as I told you no other spirit could even see the house so I was safe.'

'Could the people there see you?' Mythil asked thinking what a shock it would have been for them if Serf had suddenly appeared in their house. 'And why didn't you go to my grandfather's house?'

'No they couldn't see me and I didn't go to your grandfather's house because it has a different kind of protection. No spirit bringing danger would be allowed in. So plotting an escape route there was not an option for me,' Serf said.

'But wait a minute,' Mythil said remembering something. 'I saw Asiri in the house.'

'I never . . .' Asiri protested but Mythil interrupted.

'That's how I knew you were in trouble. I was dreaming at first but then I woke up and saw you. And you said 'Please help me. You're the only one who knows'. I saw you as clearly as I'm seeing you now.'

'But, but that can't be . . .' Asiri was puzzled. 'I mean, I was thinking those words in my head but I never came to your house.' He stopped to think. 'But wait a minute – I saw you in the same way too. Before the other yakas turned up. You suddenly appeared among the branches and said something like, 'watch out, you're in danger'. That's why I was on my guard and ready for those yakas. Even though there was nothing much I could do.' They turned to Serf looking puzzled.

The bahirawaya cleared his throat and smiled ruefully. 'After so many years of silence my throat is protesting at all this talk!' The boys laughed. Serf's voice was certainly sounding a little hoarse.

'First let's finish the story I started telling you, all right?' When the boys nodded he went on.

'Bhishani knew that I would lose power the further away from the portal I got. So she just sent some of the weaker spirits after me – of course they never found me – and the rest of them stayed behind to try and prise the ring off the rock. They succeeded too, although I believe that some of them got sucked into the vortex. For some reason Bhishani decided to hide the ring rather than destroy it.

'And that's the story of how I lost my power. I gained it again thanks to you two, but you already know that story.'

Home for breakfast

'What will you do now Serf? Now that you've got your power back?' Mythil asked. 'Will you be catching the other bad yakas and sending them through the portal? The ones that go around making slaves of others and killing humans who can see them. The ones like Bhishani. If you catch them I will be safe.'

'I understand your fear Mythil. But my place is here,' Serf said gently. 'My middle name is Serf remember?' His eyes twinkled at Mythil. 'I am bound to guard the portal.'

As Mythil hung his head in disappointment the bahirawaya went on. 'Do you remember when you first met me I asked you whether you had any powers of your own that could help you to solve your dilemma?'

'Yes, and I said no,' Mythil said dejectedly. He pulled the penknife out and turned it around in his hands. 'All I have is the knife and it's not a super power. And I can see yakas but that's what's getting me in trouble.'

'Are you sure that you don't have any other power?' Serf asked. 'And that you don't have what it takes to protect unsuspecting, unseeing people and weaker spirits from ambitious yakas like Bhishani?'

Mythil opened his mouth to say something and then shut it. How could he protect people and spirits when he was an easy target himself? Asiri voiced his thoughts.

'But he's not powerful enough. Neither of us are. If we go after bad spirits they'll just destroy us.'

'All right, let's leave that for a bit and look at something else then,' Serf said pushing his crown back again as it threatened to slide off his forehead. Mythil knew there was a smile lurking around the corners of the bahirawaya's mouth and he felt his spirits rise.

'The two of you were able to communicate with each other,' Serf said. 'Even though one of you was in the jungle and the other in a protected house. Can't you guess how that could be?'

Mythil and Asiri exchanged glances. Was that a super power? They looked at Serf and shook their heads so he went on.

'It's because you're already friends.' Seeing that the boys didn't look convinced Serf went on. 'Asiri, I don't need to tell you the power of friendship. Why do you always go in search of humans to live with?'

'It's so that I won't be alone,' Asiri said.

'Is that all?' Serf asked. 'Think carefully. How do you feel when you're with a family?'

'I feel safer,' Asiri said, groping for the right words, 'and . . . more confident . . .' He glanced at the bahirawaya. Serf was looking back at him expectantly. Asiri decided that, that wasn't the word the bahirawaya was looking for either so he scrabbled around for more words. 'I feel stronger, and . . .'

'Stronger! Exactly!' Serf exclaimed. 'When a yaka helps someone he gets stronger.'

'You mean Asiri has more power now?' Mythil asked, puzzled. 'Because he helped get the ring back? Because he tried to save my life when he could have run away?'

'Yes!' Asiri said excitedly, turning to Mythil. 'I think he's right. Try and make me change.'

'What?' Mythil asked, confused.

'Try and see my yaka face. Go on. Every time you look at me like I'm different I can't stop you from making me change . . . you know . . . from my human form.'

'Oh,' Mythil said, understanding at last. 'Ok.' He sat up straight in his hammock and looked hard at Asiri. Serf was right. Now that they were friends it was difficult to see Asiri as anything other than another boy.

Mythil relaxed his shoulders, closed his eyes and tried again. He thought of how Asiri's people had come through a portal into this world. They would have been blue wisps of smoke until the bahirawayas gave them masks. How terrified he would have been if he had seen that. Seen swarms of yakas swirling around him . . .

He opened his eyes and Asiri's eyes were glowing. But only for a moment or two. After that Asiri managed to keep his human form, grinning from ear to ear.

'I can do it!' he crowed. 'Your power's still as strong as ever but I can overcome it. I'm strong enough to do that now.'

'I think I may have lost some of it actually – some of my power as you call it,' Mythil said a little puzzled. 'I tried to make myself get as scared as I used to when I saw a yaka but I couldn't. It's like I know them now – yakas. How they came to this world and how they're just like humans in lots of ways except that they look different on the outside.'

Serf was beaming like a proud parent whose child had just topped the class. 'You haven't lost any of it Mythil. You're just beginning to understand how to control it. The key to controlling your power is to stop fearing the yakas,' he said. 'To understand that they're like your kind even though they don't look like it in their spirit form. You can do that now can't you? You're not afraid of their fearsome faces any more are you?'

'Their fearsome faces are just their masks right?' Mythil asked. 'The ones the bahirawayas made a long time ago. The ones you have in that invisible bag.'

'Exactly,' Serf said, pulling out another mask from within the silver hoop. 'They need these masks to survive.' He fused a spirit with the mask and another bewildered yaka stood before them. This one had fierce eyebrows and a mouth full of dagger like teeth but she looked quite shy and mouse-like somehow. With a tap she was sent away and Serf continued. 'But underneath it all they're like your kind. They have both the good and bad qualities of human beings.'

'Yes,' Mythil agreed. 'I think I've already learnt that. I think that's why I'm not so scared of yakas anymore.'

'You looked pretty scared a while ago,' Asiri reminded him.

Mythil remembered how terrified he had been when he and Asiri had faced Bhishani and her minions. 'Yes, well, I'd still be scared of yakas if they meant to harm me,' Mythil said. 'But not in the same way as before. I mean I would be scared of them in the way I'd be scared of my headmaster at school. But I'm not scared of yakas just because they're yakas anymore. Does that make sense?' he asked forgetting his muddy hands and scratching his head.

'Absolutely,' the bahirawaya said with a smile of satisfaction. 'I think we could say that you've got a healthy respect for them. You've discovered the key to controlling your gift. Your other super power. A combination of knowledge and friendship.'

'That means we can be friends now can't we?' Asiri asked earnestly. 'Can't we? We can look out for each other and . . . and . . .' He trailed off because Mythil seemed not to have heard him.

'So you mean that now, because I know the whole story about the yakas, I'd have to really concentrate hard to be able to see one?' Mythil asked Serf. The bahirawaya nodded solemnly.

'You've accepted the yakas now so you're not afraid of them. And, as you said, even when you do fear them it's not the sort of out of control fear you had before. The fear that forced them to change back into their yaka form. As you did with Asiri just now, you might make their eyes glow briefly but you could stop before they changed completely. And before they realised what you'd done.'

Mythil sat back in his hammock feeling giddy with relief. It was going to be all right. Everything was going to be all right.

Noticing Asiri still looking anxiously at him Mythil grinned. He swung his hammock closer to the other boy and gave him a friendly punch on the arm.

'I'm sorry I was so mean to you before,' he said as he swung away. 'Will you be my friend?'

The smile on Asiri's face mirrored his own. 'I'll need a day or two to think it over,' he said. Mythil laughed.

'See, I told you I know humans,' Asiri said. 'That was a joke and you laughed.'

'Yeah, I did,' Mythil said with a grin. 'You're a real funny guy.'

'Well, all's well that ends well. And now it's time for me to leave,' Serf told the boys.

Mythil felt a jolt of regret. He had come to trust the bahirawa lord and to feel safe when he was around. But I've got to learn to rely on myself, he thought. And my friend Asiri. Asiri grinned at Mythil's serious face and

Mythil grinned back.

'Thank you Serf,' he said. 'Thank you for teaching me how to control my power.'

'And for saving our lives,' Asiri added.

'And I thank you both,' Serf said with a bow. 'Without your bravery I would still be powerless and trapped outside the portal.' His eyes twinkled mischievously. 'You have both been brave serpent warriors,' he said.

With shrieks of laughter Mythil and Asiri grabbed handfuls of flowers and pelted Serf. Scrunching his eyes against the flying petals Mythil looked at the laughing bahirawaya and at Asiri the yaka-boy. It was good to laugh with friends, he thought.

When the flower fight was over their hammocks gently lowered themselves to within a foot of the ground. Mythil and Asiri stepped off them rather reluctantly. The hammocks melted back into the tree.

'Will it take you long to get back?' Asiri asked, nodding at the small glowing blue patch on the rock.

'I should be home in time for breakfast,' Serf said. But he was hiding a smile again and Mythil wasn't sure whether he was kidding. 'I've been away too long. I need to find out what's been happening in all that time.'

'Is there a special lady bahirawaya waiting for you, Serf?' Mythil asked mischievously. Asiri giggled hiding his teeth behind his hand.

Serf's eyes twinkled. 'I'll let you know when I get back,' he said.

It must be strange for him to go back home after so long, Mythil thought. He wondered what Serf's home was like. But the bahirawaya looked tired and Mythil thought that he'd leave that question for later.

'Now listen, I can't take the ring that opens the vortex with me when I go,' Serf said. 'So I'm entrusting it to the two of you. Only you will be able to touch it Mythil – you've seen what the metal will do to spirits. The blade of your Seeya's pen-knife is made of the same material.'

Mythil patted the knife in his pocket again and Asiri touched his arm where the knife had pierced it the day before. He certainly hadn't forgotten the pain and the way the blade had shot out blue lights.

'But how will you get back if we have the ring?' Mythil asked.

'Not to worry, I have my ways. And when I'm back I'll send you a message so that you can come back and return the ring to me. I'm sure between you two you'll think of a good plan to keep it safe till I get back. You know what kind of damage that ring can cause in the wrong hands.' The boys nodded seriously.

'And now I must be off. My world awaits me.' He tapped the ring in the rock. As the vortex opened up Serf smiled at them. 'Until we meet again,' he called out above the roaring of the vortex. Then with a jaunty salute he stepped into the swirling blue light and disappeared.

'See you later Serf!' Mythil yelled into the blue glare of the portal. He and Asiri watched the vortex grow smaller and smaller until there was just the ring in the rock. It fell off with a clink and a splash on to the rainwater filled charred clay lamps at the foot of the rock.

Now that the light from the vortex no longer filled the clearing and the protection of the force field had disappeared Mythil realised that the rain had stopped and dawn was breaking. A bird was chirping somewhere in the silence. Mythil bent down to pick up the ring. He wiped it on his t-shirt, which was quite dry now though streaked with crusty mud like the rest of him, and slipped it carefully into his pocket.

He and Asiri stood in silence for a while listening as more and more birds began to join the morning chorus. Then quite suddenly Mythil yawned. It was a huge yawn. He couldn't help himself. He felt so tired. But more than anything else he felt happy. He breathed in the earthy smell of the rain sodden jungle and sighed.

'Come on, let's go home,' Mythil said, putting a muddy arm around Asiri's shoulders.

'Home,' Asiri breathed with a beaming smile. 'I've waited so long for a place to call home. I can't believe it's happening.'

Mythil stopped in his tracks. 'Um . . . but my family doesn't believe me. They don't think yakas are real so we won't be able to tell them. You won't mind being invisible around them will you? You can still be invisible right?' Asiri grinned at Mythil before disappearing. It felt odd to have his arm around someone he couldn't see.

'No problem,' Asiri said and Mythil sighed in relief. 'You won't exactly have a family. But you'll have a friend. Is that okay?'

'A friend? Who? Jamis?' Asiri asked and Mythil punched him.

'Me, silly,' he said.

'You, silly, are fine,' Asiri said with a chuckle. 'Can we come back here and play tomorrow?' he asked making himself visible again.

'It's already tomorrow,' Mythil said trying to stifle another yawn.

'So it is,' Asiri said. 'Today then, after you've rested?'

Mythil smiled, 'Yeah, that'll be great. And when term starts you can come to school with me. Imagine the pranks we can play in class with you invisible!' he said.

'Oh I'm good at pranks!' Asiri said pulling an overhanging branch and soaking Mythil in rainwater.

'I know,' Mythil said shoving him into the middle of a rain-drenched bush. 'There's going to be hard work too though. We'll have to practice our powers so we can work together like a team to help Serf.'

'But there'll be plenty of time to play too right?' Asiri asked as they crossed the stream together.

'Plenty of time,' Mythil agreed thinking that the next time he was told to go outside and play he'd actually have someone to play with. He clapped Asiri on the shoulder. 'It's going to be fun,' he said and grinning happily the boys headed home.

The End